GRIM PORTRAITS

SIX STORIES ABOUT THE DARK SIDE OF ART

KEALAN PATRICK BURKE

GRIM PORTRAITS

Six Stories About the Dark Side of Art

Kealan Patrick Burke

Cover Design by Elderlemon Design

Elderlemon Press

ISBN: 9798861140379

To all my fellow creatives in these dark times of devalued and depreciated art.
Never stop.

CONTENTS

INTRODUCTION

I'm addicted to art. Put me in a gallery and leave me there forever. I'll wander for hours peering into works that are not just a fusion of paints and pigment, but windows into someone else's imagination. I'm as fascinated by paintings as I am by books and movies and videogames. All of them are canvases of a storyteller's mind.

Once upon a time, I brought my stepson to a local community art gallery. He was enthralled by the works on display, many of them rudimentary efforts by burgeoning artists still honing their craft, but one of them stopped him in his tracks. It was a crude watercolor of an orange with a plain white background. I admit to being puzzled by its effect on him, a picture I found quite basic and plain, so I asked him what it was he saw in it.

"Textures," he replied. "When I first looked at it, I saw an orange."

"And what do you see now?"

"Universes."

If there's a better analogy for the artistic experience, I don't know what it is.

* * *

Some years later, his uncle Adam came to visit us in the farmhouse in which we lived at the time.

While upstairs shaving himself in the old oval mirror above the bathroom sink, the glass slipped out of the frame and shattered. It was not until Adam raised his eyes to the mirror frame, still hanging on the wall, that he realized someone was looking back at him.

It was a charcoal portrait of a stern old man, his name scrawled at the bottom, barely legible, but enough for us to make out "Colonel William".

Our subsequent research revealed that the man had been a military man of some regard from southern Ohio.

At some point, his portrait had ended up in a yard sale and whomever purchased it decided to use the frame for a mirror with the portrait as the backing. An odd idea, perhaps, but I don't proclaim to know anything about interior design. That portrait was dated October 1928.

October.

Season of the dead.

In the weeks that followed, that portrait moved around our house without anyone laying a hand on it. We'd prop it up against the baseboard downstairs and return from errands to find it back upstairs hanging on the nail above the bathroom sink. We put it in the basement and came back to find it on the kitchen table covered in cobwebs. Now, you'd be hard-pressed to find a bigger skeptic than me, but I admit it gave me the creeps (even if I suspected it was my stepson behind it all, though he swore on a stack of Bibles he had nothing to do with it because he said he'd rather have burned it than go anywhere near it.)

Then one night, while my wife and I were watching TV, we heard the sound of someone clapping upstairs, followed by the rush of children's footsteps on the stairs themselves, as if they were obeying a command. The sound was so sharp and clear, I fully expected to see a pair of chastened children rounding the stairs to appear in our living room.

No one did, of course.

By then, I'd had enough of this weirdness, and decided it was time for us to be rid of the portrait, so I did what all young enterprising folk (read: broke young writers) with possibly paranormal ephemera do: I put it up on eBay, with the story I've just told you attached.

In the end, I think it went for about $350 to a collector of the paranormal in Florida. Not bad for something that had hidden itself behind glass for countless years until it revealed itself to our startled Adam.

A condition of the sale was that whoever bought it should keep in touch and let me know if they experienced anything. The buyer agreed, but I never heard from him again. Soon after the sale, his emails bounced, and when I looked up his address a few months later, his house was under someone else's name.

All very mysterious, but also, very explainable. I just don't happen to have an explanation, nor do I even care to think about that portrait much, because in truth, whenever I do, it's not those events I think about, but the image of that sour old face staring at the back of the mirror all those years, maybe seeing *through* it, watching us go about our lives, perhaps jealously. And it always gives me a shudder.

If this was a fictional story, I would have that old man making his way back from Florida, perhaps traveling from mirror to mirror until he finds me again and makes me pay for trying to be rid of him.

Shudder.

* * *

Everyone remembers *The Twilight Zone*. For many of us, it was the start of our love affair with horror and science fiction. Fewer people remember the series Rod Serling did afterward, the short-lived *Night Gallery*, which was more horror than science fiction and featured stories by such luminaries as H.P. Lovecraft, Basil Copper, August Derleth, Charles Wandrei, Fritz Leiber, and a great many by Serling himself. Not to be outdone by his evocative introductions on *The Twilight Zone*, *Night Gallery* starts with Serling in an art gallery, unveiling the paintings that form the basis of the stories to follow:

Good evening, and welcome to a private showing of three paintings, displayed here for the first time. Each is a collector's item in its own way—not because of any special artistic quality, but because each captures on a canvas, suspended in time and space, a frozen moment of a nightmare.

And I loved that. The paintings too (by Thomas J. Wright and Jaroslav Gebr) were appropriately chilling, as were most of the stories, particularly Charles Beaumont's "The Howling Man", which lived in my brain for many a sleepless night. But as with many of the older horror shows, time dulls their impact, even as they take their places in the gallery of our fondest memories.

Nevertheless, it was *Night Gallery* and its impact on me back in the day that inspired this latest collection of insidious horrors, all of which are in one way or another connected to art.

These stories were a great deal of fun to write, and I hope they're as much fun to read. If you enjoy them, or even if you don't, please bear in mind I once dated an artist of strange paintings she claimed were a combination of cellular biology and cosmic interference. Her paintings were unique and incredible, but made my head hurt if I looked at them too long, and I maintain to this day, they unlocked a door inside my head through which all manner of evils spill forth.

If you're lucky, you'll get through these grim portraits with your sanity intact.

If not, I'll see you on the other side of the frame.

SOMETIMES THEY SEE ME

1

I met Calvin on the Singing Bridge outside Rosewood Park on the night of December 24th. I'd gone there to kill myself, and though he never admitted it, so had he. It was there in his eyes, the same flat look of grim resignation I'm sure I carried in mine. Everyone goes there to die. It's become a cliché, but such things don't matter where the end of your life is concerned.

He'd been throwing scraps of paper down into the frozen water. The scene looked familiar to me, but it would take a while before I could recall where I had seen it before. In that moment, I was more intrigued by his posture and the aura radiating from his emaciated body.

"I can wait," were my first words to him, and his response bound us together until the end of the whole mess.

"For how long?"

The night was full of funny things, the first of them being that when I rounded the spiderweb of frozen trees and saw his dark figure hunched over the railing in the haze of cold moonlight, I felt a brief twinge of panic, the same kind any woman feels when she finds herself unexpectedly alone with a stranger. That I worried he might be a killer only tickled me later as we lay in bed together reminiscing on how fucked up it all was. If he'd turned out to be a homicidal maniac, it would have put a serious damper on my plan to kill myself. But that's the interesting thing about suicide. It's a personal thing, perhaps the *most* personal thing of all, the very last measure of control. Thus, having someone else do it doesn't count. Instinct will revolt if the executioner isn't you.

Rather than cast our bodies into the freezing current, we walked and talked, and retreated to his place among the unsteady tenement buildings in a part of town nobody thinks of as anything but a backdrop to the occasional nameless murder on the nightly news. There on the second floor, by the cozy light of a host of guttering candles, we drank cheap vodka, laughed, and wept and entered each other both spiritually and physically until sleep left us entwined in his stained and stinking sheets.

With his true nature written in sweat all over my skin, my dreams did not, for the first time in years, try to drown me in anxiety. I did not see the wallpaper, and I did not see the blood. I saw only magic.

I *knew* him.

And so, our brief love story began.

2

One of my late father's truisms, deposed while bribing me out of his life: You're only fine until you tell on yourself. Aside from the most remarkable of them, a few more of Calvin's truths became evident early on. He was an alcoholic and an addict, manic depressive, and possibly a narcissist. I don't know how long we meandered through those drunken days before I realized I knew more about him than he did me. That was because I asked questions, whereas he was content to let me be a mystery. Or maybe he didn't care. I guess the nature of your passenger doesn't alter the destination, and we were on the road now, familiars, headed somewhere together, even if the motion was an illusion. Our days saw us waking in his grimy, powerless apartment, fucking like we'd die if we didn't, barely bathing beneath the teardrop trickle of cold water in the calamitous bathroom, and eschewing breakfast in favor of whiskeys at a local dive bar, The Big Grand, a disproportionately austere name for a place where your feet stick to the floor and the regulars are only marginally more material than shadow.

From there, we walked the cobblestoned streets and ambled aimlessly through the nicer part of town, cackling when we found ourselves obstructing the urgency of the better-dressed and daring each other to antagonize the police whenever we caught them giving us the rooster eye. Bookstores and libraries provided succor, a spiritual peace that saw us return to something almost human, cowed by the awe of a hundred thousand voices clamoring to be heard above the din of reverent quiet. Only here could we be apart, like sinners to the confessionals that best suited our brand of sin, baring our souls without judgment before a godless jury.

Afterward, better educated, we reunited, rejuvenated by dead men's tales and hidden knowledge, and off out into the world we went again in search of more distraction from the ever-encroaching edge of the inevitable abyss.

Running beneath it all was an awareness of doom, of borrowed time, and of the secrets we were keeping from each other.

It would end, this little adventure, and probably not well.

3

On the last of our jaunts into the city, three weeks since we first met, we stopped before the large plate-glass window of The Orchid Gallery. It was nestled between a secondhand bookstore and a Subway, within which, the employees stared out at us in an envy unique to the bored and underpaid. Displayed before us in the gallery window were a series of small paintings apparently floating in thin air against a backdrop of stark white. Each canvas depicted an explosion of colors in no discernible pattern, the kind of work Pollock was known for, only less agitated, and no less impenetrable. There was a softness to it that appealed to me, even though such art has always seemed to me at best nonsensical, at worst constrictive, even while it inspires paroxysms of desire among aficionados. How difficult is it to spackle a canvas in fury, and what is it we're supposed to see other than orgiastic chaos? But perhaps that's just me. I have an aversion to art I have never quite been able to reconcile beyond its tendency to constrain. How can such things move us when they require us to stand still? What is it they're supposed to say? I divine no more emotion from a slapdash mosaic of paint than I do a pile of coats on a floor.

"It's wondrous," Calvin said, and I watched my reflection

second his appraisal with a treasonous nod.

We went inside. The gallery was one long narrow room with walls of white-painted brick and a lot less art than one would expect given the purpose of the place. Even the art that was there embraced too much negative space to the point that the sparse amounts of color seemed like an oversight.

One of the paintings caught Calvin's eye and held it. It was a small blue square in the center of an enormous rectangular canvas. Within the square was a single red thumbprint. A simple placard beneath read: *"Identity" – by Doris Wiltshire.* Beneath that, the price. *$17,000.*

"Are they fucking serious?"

Calvin ignored me, still enthralled, and I couldn't help but wonder at the source of his fascination. I lingered dutifully until ants began to crawl their way out of my bones, and then I went outside for a cigarette.

Three cigarettes later, my patience expired. I needed a fix or a drink, preferably both, and Calvin was burning our time staring down a fucking thumbprint. It no longer mattered what it meant to him. Only the need mattered now, and he was its sole obstruction. When I looked through the window, I saw him turn to say something to me. Only then did it dawn on him that I wasn't there. His gaunt, pockmarked face screwed up in bafflement before our gazes met through the glass, mine hot enough to warp it. He nodded and hurried out to join me.

"The fuck was that about?" I asked him, my irritation evident in everything from my tone to the way I stomped my cigarette to death on the pavement, an act which gleaned a look of disapproval from a woman hustling her two oblivious children along before us. "And what the fuck are *you* looking at?" I feel bad about that. It wasn't her fault that she reminded me of my sister.

Calvin took my elbow and led us to the closest bar. He handed me a baggy and shoved me into the bathroom, where he went down on me while I shot up, and we were fine again for a little while. I didn't climax, but that's nothing new.

4

"I wanted to be an artist for the longest time, ever since my parents took me to Atlantic City and I saw those guys doing caricatures on the boardwalk. I was enthralled by them. Couldn't stop watching them. Couldn't move. Would have stayed there forever. These working joes getting to sit outside with the smells of the sea and the popcorn and hotdogs, painting likenesses of people all day long. Took me years to realize I wasn't very good and never would be, though I was featured for a while in The Vanderelli Room. People seemed to like it and it excited me to be so positively appraised. I thought I might be going places, but I couldn't make the spark catch again. I felt trapped, so I moved, thought a new space might serve me better. Thought I might be able to make a living from it someday. The self-delusion of all budding creatives. We should be compensated fairly for our passions, shouldn't we? And if the world deems art should be free, then I propose that so too should living."

I didn't respond because I knew there wouldn't be time before he started rambling again. Besides, he wouldn't have heard my answer even if I'd cared enough about the subject to offer one.

"But then I started to feel tired all the time. And down. Started to feel nervous over nothing. Couldn't get out of bed. Didn't want to. Couldn't paint. Felt like I was disappearing."

This at least was more interesting, a thread of commonality to which I could relate. I was quite adept at disappearing and the terror of unbecoming. It's why I still check my skin for the faded floral patterns of the wallpaper from my childhood home. "It's frustrating, worse than the notion of death."

"What is?"

"The idea of never being good at life."

We ordered more drinks. I was floating above myself by then, tethered to my body by some biological arrangement to which I'd not been privy and trapped in the room by the distant engine drone of his words.

"A man bit me once," I said, simply because the words had been burdening my throat.

He'd been in the middle of his mournful pontificating but stopped to consider my words. "Bit you?"

"Former lover. Blind date. Hopeless alcoholic. Woke up at his place in the middle of night and found him chewing on my arm." I roll up the right sleeve of my denim shirt to show him the oval ring of white em-dashes. "He woke with a craving for more alcohol and had none in the house, so he decided to siphon it from my veins."

"Jesus. What did you do?"

"I clawed out one of his eyes."

"Seriously?"

It felt like I was talking to him underwater, my words

slow, emerging from my mouth like delicate brush strokes. "Left him there screaming. Don't even know if he survived it or just bled to death in the bed. I took the eye. Had it encased in Lucite. I keep it on my nightstand as a reminder to be cautious among men who don't know themselves."

"Woah."

My grin feels like my face is made of butter and I'm gently scoring it with a knife. "I'm kidding."

"About the eye?"

"The biting part was real. I figure it was some fucked up fetish. The rest is the kind of thing you think of later when you're safe and it's too late to act on it."

I could tell he didn't believe any of it, but I didn't care. What was it all but words to fill a silence that didn't need filling? I wanted to fuck and sleep and get high and die, and none of that mattered either. If art requires you to be still, then life demands motion, given that there's far more of one than the other. We were cohorts in a heist, he and I, thrown together by our strange natures and mutual ambivalence for life, stealing whatever perfunctory moments of joy we could find amid the ruins of the world. There would be no consequences or penalties. We hadn't ended our lives, not yet, but inevitably we would, which freed us from the prison of obligation.

"I miss the rush," he said then, and even without knowing the flavor to which he referred, I agreed. No rush is the same, and the first is always the best. Get clean and come back to it and it's like an angel is screwing your brain. There's no guilt, no shame. That comes later when you come down or when a well-meaning Samaritan decides to adopt your burden. You feel bad because they feel bad, not because you actually regret letting the angel fuck you.

"When I paint, I become someone else. Something else. I like what it makes me even if I don't have a name for it. But I can't do it anymore and it's left a void in me I only know how to fill with bad things."

"'Bad' is a relative term though, wouldn't you say?'"

By then, I was starting to return to myself, prematurely brought down by the counterweight of his melancholy, and it was getting old. We needed a change of venue, a change of high. My elbows and toes were starting to tickle from the dust of inertia. I looked around at the long rectangular room, built to mimic a train car, if Union Pacific had a habit of filling their cars with neon beer signs, Christmas lights, old TVs showing nothing but Keno numbers and NASCAR, cheap tables, bar stools with ripped red leather for seats, and admitted only the dangerous and disadvantaged. There was an old glass rotisserie too close to the bathroom door, within which flaccid hot dogs turned like the vacant fingers of a wet rubber glove. A large woman with dirty blond hair wearing a T-shirt bearing the legend ALL LIVES MATTER looked up from her game of pool and glared a challenge in my direction, cue held rifle-like by her side. As I had no intention of getting into it with anyone brave enough to stand so close to the forty-year-old franks, I returned my attention to Calvin.

"Towards the end, I started seeing things in the paintings. The stories behind them."

"I thought that was the point of art?"

He ignored me. "Instead of photographs, I saw the people

who took the picture. Instead of paint, I saw the inspiration through the eyes of the artist. Often, it was wonderful to behold. I saw incredible things. I traveled through time, awoke in strange beds, walked unknown roads. I became other people in places alien to me. But it was not always so benevolent. Sometimes I saw terrible things. And toward the end, when it got really bad, sometimes *they* saw *me*."

"Who's 'they'?"

He looked down at his empty drink and shook his head. "If I knew that, I suppose I'd know the true meaning of art, like seeing the face of God, but I don't."

It was getting late, and I was getting bored, so I punched him on the arm to jar him from his reverie. "Let's blow this joint."

"We should go home. I'm tired. Worn down to ash by the pretense of being human, of being sane, of being, period."

I rose, the chair legs barking like a startled dog. "Fuck that. We're young. The night's young. Let's wreck it."

He looked up at me then and there was such a naked fear in his eyes it gave me pause, penetrated the protective veil of my high and twisted my guts. It's a look better suited to my own reflection on the bad nights: the atavistic dread, the misery and desperation, the absolute fear that you've reached the end of the road, and all that's left is for someone to make it official.

I didn't allow the recognition of his fear to take root. If I did, I'd be forced to join him in his dull introspective meandering, and I was too restless. I needed to keep moving, keep going, keep the high alive, or risk having my nerves exposed to my own reality. If the face of Calvin's God was art, then the face of mine was Chaos, raw and bleeding, filling the sky in a universe of my own design. Looking upon it was to risk going mad, and I was always never less than halfway there. It demanded I look, but I couldn't. Not yet.

I braced my hands flat on the table on both sides of his empty glass. My hair hung in my face, and I could smell the grease. "Look. You're having a moment. I get it. Your life didn't work out the way you thought it would. Welcome to the suck. We're both fucked, and that's fine. This rollercoaster doesn't go in reverse, so what say we ditch the self-pity and finish the ride? We're still here, you and me, primed for adventure, and if sometimes they see you, so what? I'm seeing you now and what I see is potential." I leaned over and kissed his whiskey lips. "What say we don't waste it?"

Now that the decision to leave had been made, the clamor from the bar beyond the radius of our table rushed back in, as if we'd been encased in a bubble all night.

"Hey," the barman bellowed at us, and in his meaty hands he strangled tapwater into the sink from a frayed, once-white dish rag as if were our necks. "Order a drink or get the hell out. You two have been sitting there dry for, like, over an hour now."

"Have we, *like*, been sitting here, *like*, for an over an hour? I just finished my drink, you fucking putz." I admit I was offended that somehow, in this squalid shit pit, we were the offensive ones, so I threw him a glare and kicked my chair back from the table. "We're leaving. Got reservations at a place that doesn't smell like your mother's ass."

The barman's long face turned the color of a pickled beet. "My mother's dead, you junkie bitch."

"Then it probably smells even worse."

Calvin's chuckle was the sound of a bathtub draining.

The toothless and ferociously bearded old man who had spent the greater part of the evening openly ogling my breasts from his corner of the bar called out, "Might not want to be drivin' drunk. Police're everywhere." His rubbery lips spread in a wide empty grin, exposing a tongue paler than a sundried dog turd. "I could give y'all a ride. 'Specially the lady." He cackled and I thrust a middle finger at him as the barman rounded the bar like a tornado.

Calvin shoved the door open, and we staggered out on a wave of laughter into the chill night air.

5

What followed is hazy: snapshots of pulsating lights and music, of altercations and raised voices, of broken glass and an irate Uber driver throwing us out somewhere short of our destination, of more raucous laughter, of fucking in the rain, of running from the police, and the taste of paint on my tongue. Eventually we found our way to a shitty motel, the neon light a beacon for sleaze like us. We had no pills, no coke, no heroin, but we had a bottle of cheap vodka and that would have to do until we had the presence of mind to formulate a proper score. There were tears, of course, from Calvin, who, in the absence of whirling lights and adrenaline, returned to his ennui.

"I don't know who I am. I don't know what I'm doing here."

"Does anyone?" My nose was burning and my veins felt hollow. I considered getting off the bed and just fucking him senseless if only to shut him up, but that required an effort of which I was incapable, and I wasn't sure he'd be up to it, so I busied myself with taping up the smoke alarm so I could have a cigarette. "Hey, how come you don't have any paintings at your place? Any of yours, I mean. I'd like to see some."

"I destroyed them all. Hardest thing I've ever done, but it needed to be done. It was a kind of cleansing. I hoped it would help."

"And did it?"

"A little. Not enough. Can I tell you something?"

"Anything, mi amore."

"I know why this is happening to me. I know why I can see things in the paintings that other people can't. I know why I can step through them into those worlds and see what the people who painted them saw. And I know why I'm being punished for it too."

I dropped down onto the bed and mumbled around my cigarette. "Good. Closure's good."

"It's because of my mother."

"Isn't it always? Mine used to slam me into the walls and force me to stare at the patterns on the wallpaper. If you're wondering why my nose looks like this, now you know."

"I'm sorry."

"Don't be. It was good for me. Opened my eyes to things."

"Like what?"

"Who we are beyond the artifice."

He swept his hair out of his eyes, which were gleaming.

I've seen that look in the mirror many times before.

"Yes, yes, that's it exactly. I see things now because my mother used to make me stare at her paintings until I saw what she wanted me to see in them." He nodded at the picture on the far wall by the door. Housed in a cheap brown frame, it was a drab, acrylic picture of a farmhouse and barn. "She would have torn that one off the wall. Bad art disgusted her. She agonized over her work. Sometimes I think it's what killed her. It used to drive her mad that she couldn't properly nurture her work into being. Even when she sold them and they were received well, she said they were unfinished. She said the same of all her work. She hated it. And I feel that hate, still. It lives in me because I've never been able to shake the sense that she felt the same about me: an unfinished disappointment."

I was starting to get tired. It had been a long day, my system jolted by so many drugs while being softened by too much alcohol. My heart didn't know what to do with itself, so it was time to let it rest before it decided to quit.

"She made me stare at them for hours. I used to make up things I saw in them to keep her happy."

"That's nice. You were a good kid."

"I did it for so long and so often I started seeing the paintings move. It made me ill. I was sick for a long time. My mother got sick too. Cancer. She had my father set up an easel in her room, but not for her. It was for me. She wanted me to paint her, to preserve her suffering. She wanted me to be an artist. I didn't yet know how, so I couldn't paint her. I was terrified I would disappoint her. But I forced it, and what emerged was the kind of effort you'd expect from a twelve-year-old. After the last stroke was done, I turned the easel around to show it to her, but she was dead." He shrugged, picked at the dead white skin on his big toe. "I don't blame her. I loved her. She just wanted people to be able to see what she saw, so they could understand her, but she couldn't get the images right. Which means no matter how her work was celebrated, she died a stranger to the world. The same will happen to me."

"The same happens to everyone. Even if you're known in life, we're all strangers in death."

"It feels like my time's coming."

I don't like when the conversation turns this way, as it so often does among people like us. There's always a moment in which you decide you've had enough of being nothing, that it's time to put the eraser down before you vanish completely, that you're finally ready to make a fresh start. The problem with that resolution is that it's like deciding to build a house because you know where to find a hammer. The tool is nothing without the materials and the will. If you allow the vow to take hold, it becomes a bogeyman, terrifying in its implications, so to prepare for it, you make a ceremony over having one last bump, one last high, and that reminds you how ill-prepared you are for anything else. *Why in holy fuck would you ever want to face the world clean?* you think. But, if by some miracle you come out of it with your determination intact, where do you begin? Rehab? Here's the funny thing about rehab: it's full of people who smile and tell their stories and congratulate each other and applaud and give out coins and then walk back out into the world with no idea what to do with themselves. Maybe they have a nice 9-5 job, a supportive wife, some kids. None of that can expel the nagging feeling that something's missing from you, something's not right. It's as if some mad surgeon crept into your house and removed one of your lungs while you slept. You live in a state of perpetual dissatisfaction, of being a passenger on the wrong train looking longingly out the window at all the happy people traveling the right one. For no good reason, you randomly find it difficult to breathe. You have no friends who aren't junkies. You become an expert at spotting people who are carrying, and they're the angels beckoning a return to the fold. It's grief, it's mourning, and there's only one way to cure it. It's why they call it a fix.

So no, I didn't want to have this conversation now. Or ever. A day might come in which I turn a similar corner, decide to get my shit in order. But that's not today, and it's not tomorrow, and it's none of your fucking business.

I threw back the covers and patted a hand on the bed next to me. "Come on, lover. Come to bed."

"I can't stop walking into those paintings," he said then. "But the last time...the night I met you on the bridge...that was the worst of all."

He rose unsteadily, and that was progress. His pupils were small periods on a page streaked with thin red lines. A bead of sweat hung suspended from his stubbled chin.

"Why's that?"

He pulled his shirt up over his head and the bones in his chest were like kindling beneath a dirty white sheet.

"Because I almost forgot how to get back out."

6

Even under oath, I'll never admit to being an addict or an alcoholic, no more than I'd swear to have either habit under control. No denial for this girl, no, siree. Just evasion. I prefer to think myself caught somewhere in the middle, a woman without a country but with periodic access to GPS if I ever want it. Weeks go by in which I don't take anything, and hardly touch the booze. Calvin called it Jilting the Dragon. It's good to jilt the dragon every once in a while, even if just to prove that I can, to engage in a brief reminder of what it's like to be back behind the wheel of my own life. But those are also the worst times, dark and frightening times, and I don't much care for them. The world thinks being clean is the respectable way to be, but it's also the hardest. Sobriety is a world of sharp edges and pain, and I will never understand why you wouldn't avoid it if you had the choice.

Andrea, my younger sister, wants nothing to do with me. No doubt she tells herself it's because I'm an addict. She acts embarrassed by me, though I've never given her any reason to feel this way. I've never done her wrong. The beating heart of the enmity between us then, has more to do with how she feels every time she thinks of me, not as an adult, but a child. My memories of her are bittersweet. For a time, we were close, but the schism began once my mother began to physically abuse me (initially I misspelled that as *psychically*, but I guess that's even more apt). To Andrea, my mother showed only love, and no sign of the abject hatred which one day materialized out of thin air. While I was getting my nose broken, or beaten with a wooden spoon, or being dragged by my hair along the hallway floor, Andrea was in the living room, pretending to watch TV, while watching our reflections on the screen. She has no reason to hate me, nor do I hate her, but I clearly remember feeling that our bond withered a little bit more every time I asked myself why she had escaped my mother's wrath, why I'd been chosen as the target of her fury. In my darkest moments, I felt an impulse to bestow upon my sister the same violence bestowed upon me, perhaps as a means of restoring some perverse balance, but I didn't have it in me. I think now she wants nothing to do with me because I'm a walking reminder that if not for me, the sacrificial lamb, her world would have been very different. There is, of course no way of knowing if this is true. Any hope of divining such information would require us talking, and we don't do that. The deep cracks in our relationship are destined to remain unshored.

Perhaps because Andrea and the past had been on my mind, once Calvin and I finally turned in, I dreamt of my mother, and of that horrid wallpaper, and of blood pattering my shoes. Jazz music drifted down from upstairs where my father had sequestered himself in his study with a bottle of bourbon and his own cowardice. I began to turn my head in the feeble hope that if she saw the terror on my face it might wake her up, and my mother grabbed a fistful of my hair.

"Do you know what you are, you little cunt?" she shrieked at me. She was weaving on her feet so badly it was like we were engaged in a peculiar waltz. The medication did not make her this monster. The as-yet undiagnosed degenerative brain disorder did that. But really, to my nine-year-old self, the reasons mattered little. I just didn't want to be afraid and in pain.

I heard the tiniest little sob from the living room, almost lost beneath the nickelodeon soundtrack of some cartoon. It didn't come again.

"You're a horrible, ugly, soulless leech," my mother shrieked at me, and shoved my face into the wall. The pattern filled my vision, became a world lit by disintegrating stars. I felt an explosion of pain and heard an awful dull crunch inside my skull as my nose broke.

All because I burned the eggs.

7

When I woke, I could still smell them and for a moment, I thought of screaming, until the red neon flashed into the motel room and brought me back to myself. I was covered in sweat, my default state these days, the sodden blankets like plaster of Paris setting around my legs. In the process of freeing myself, I realized Calvin was not beside me.

"Hey," I said to the red-veined dark. "Where'd you go?"

When he didn't answer, I figured he was either in the bathroom, or had stepped outside for a cigarette. I slid out of bed, my head filled with sand, mouth with glue, and my stomach lurched as the night inside me looked for a way out. I hurried to the bathroom. It was dark. As I flicked on the dim light, I wondered if Calvin was outside, or maybe had gone to score. This last would have suited me fine. In my experience, nothing halts the onset of the dreaded morning after better than a chemical extension. It's why alcoholics always keep a few beers in the fridge and vampires sleep in coffins. It's a protective measure against unwanted intrusion.

Eyes shut, I let the stream of urine loose. I was weaving on the seat, in danger of falling back asleep right there, but then a sound from the other side of the bathroom wall permeated the fog and I opened one eye, squinting against the fluorescent light. When I cocked my head slightly to better hear the sound, my gaze fell upon the sink, which was close enough for me to hit with my elbow in the confines of the squalid room.

The basin was spattered with blood.

And now, despite the still developing hangover and exhaustion, I was awake. I finished peeing, dabbed myself dry, and pulled up my panties. "Calvin?"

No answer.

Worried, I splashed some cold water on my face, which washed away the Rorschach pattern of blood in the basin. The iciness of it shocked air into my lungs but brought with it the level of alertness required for an impromptu nocturnal investigation.

"Calvin? You up?"

I did not look at myself in the mirror. I try to avoid that as much as possible. Reflections are inveterate liars.

I left the light on and the door open so I could see the bed. It was still empty but for a cumulonimbus of wrinkled sheets, but now I could hear a swishing, scratching sound from the living room-cum-kitchen, or whatever the fuck you call those claustrophobic areas in motel rooms that aren't the bed.

The room was lit only by the intermittent hazy red light from the neon sign. Backlit by the light from the bathroom, I saw a distorted version of myself in the cheap television screen and thought of Andrea trying hard not to be aware of the horror. Beyond it, just beside the door to the room, Calvin was a hazy, agitated, and indistinct shape.

"What are you doing?"

"Working."

"Are you okay? There was blood in the sink."

"It's not blood. It's paint. I needed red."

His hands were pale smudges in the gloom, moving like spiders over the painting of the rustic barn.

"It's late. Come back to bed."

"Do you know where this is?"

I folded my arms. Now that I knew he wasn't bleeding to death, I just wanted to go back to bed. "Where what is?"

"This barn. Do you know where the barn in this painting is?"

"No. How would I know that?"

"Have you never stepped into the painting to see for yourself?"

"Can't say that I have, no."

"I've painted a door in it for you if you'd like to see."

"I'm going back to bed."

"It's in a place called Rowan County in North Carolina. The man who owned the barn shot his wife and daughter six months after painting this picture."

"Calvin, come on. Come back to bed. Whatever you're doing, you can finish it in the morning. Let's get some sleep."

A great sadness fell over me at the thought of losing him. I'd known it was coming. I'd just hoped it would take longer.

The scratching and swishing continued. The cheap frame

of the painting clattered against the wall. And then his voice, lower and slower than I'd ever heard it, the kind of voice a man gets when he's smoked too much and drunk too little, crept its way across the room.

"He swore in court he didn't do it, and he meant it too. He couldn't remember doing any of it. Couldn't remember staking their bodies up in the cornfield either, which was how he got caught. Guy next door came by to see how his neighbor had managed to make those scarecrows look so damn lifelike and yurked up his breakfast right then and there. Ran screaming back to his house and called the police. When they took John McAllister away, he said somebody with a grudge must have framed him. Get it? Somebody framed the artist."

The swishing scratching sound stopped.

Thank God for small mercies.

"They executed him. Framed and hanged like fine art."

"Why are you telling me this?"

He turned and his eyes were black holes. "You've been keeping things from me."

So here we were, our moment come. I'd wanted it to be so much different, but now I realize there's no way it ever could have been. From the very beginning, this was its natural end.

"I would have told you, if you'd asked, but you never did," I said.

I watched him limp toward me. One of his feet was broken and hanging at an odd angle, but he expressed no pain.

"You poor thing."

"What is this?" he asked me. "What have you done to me?"

It wasn't darkness that hid his eyes from me. He had either painted them black, or they had been removed. Through his pale skin, his veins were black as winter trees and appeared to be moving, as if wrenched by the force of a subcutaneous storm. The shape of his body made no visual sense anymore. His bones, his joints, had come out of true and his skin rippled and bulged and twisted as if he were made of plastic. When he stepped into the light from the bathroom, I saw that his wrists were broken too, which explained why he'd stopped defacing the barn. His hands hung like dead flowers from the withered stalks of his arms.

"Tell me," he said, sounding as if he was gargling blood. "Tell me what you've done."

"I will, love," I told him. "But first please understand that I have done nothing to you. I'm only here to make the end a little better."

8

On the day my mother first slammed me into the wall, I detached from myself, went *through* the wall, and it was real. I was there, trapped in the narrow space between the walls. I could see the wooden framework, the wires, the cobwebs, the mice, and when I looked up, I could see through the floor to where my father sat weeping at his desk. I could see inside him, and it was all gray, like a sky considering rain.

I am, or at least for a time I was, reasonable and sane enough to believe that what I experienced as a child, being able to see the mechanics behind the skin of things, was most likely delusional, a reaction to sudden trauma, or a psychological escape tactic. I told myself this for ten years before going to court-ordered rehab for alcohol after my first DUI. There, a sponsor named Stephen Carver became my guru. He encouraged me to allow myself to believe in the spiritual benefit of healing, to be open to other realms and possibilities. One of the possibilities I didn't predict was him trying to stick his hand down my pants on the one and only night I let him drive me home. I broke his nose, blackened his eye, cut off his dick and rammed it up his ass, all in my mind on the walk home after he threw me out of his car. But as I raged, ashamed at what he had almost done to me, shaking in fear of where that might have led, I saw him as if he had appeared right back in front of me. I saw *inside* him, from the liquor boiling in his stomach to the splintering of his bones, the perforation of organs, the collapsing of his skull, as his car collided with a snowplow. That didn't happen, of course.

Not that night.

It happened the winter of the next year. *So, wow, you can see the future, huh?* I hear you ask while rolling your eyes. *How come you're not a TV celebrity? How many books have you written off the back of this amazing superpower? When is the world tour?* The short answer is that it isn't a power at all. It's a lens, and one that only works when I'm high, just like I was the night I failed to miss all the creepy vibes Carver was giving me. It was the reason I'd called him in the first place. *I'm fucked up and I need help. I don't feel real and I keep thinking my mother is coming for me.* And anything that only happens when you're high only makes sense to fellow users. Should I have donned a cape and told Stephen Carver he might die by snowplow sometime in the future? He'd have laughed and tried to finish what he started.

I let whatever this ability or hex is fade into insignificance as time went on, and if sometimes I knew little things about people they might not have wanted me to know: from their sexual proclivities and secrets to the fate awaiting them years hence, I put it down to the heightened perception any addict can claim because it's hard to disprove. If I told you were going to die in a plane crash somewhere and then it happened in eight years' time, would you think to credit the source? Of course not. You'd be deader than hammered shit. Anyone else who might have heard such a pronouncement surely wouldn't remember the one night some homeless looking heroin addict spouted wisdom from the stoop while you were walking by. When asked, I can't predict jack. When it could be most useful, it doesn't come. Why not parlay it into a means of the perfect score, you ask? Why didn't I rob a bank, buy myself a mansion, pull one over on a dealer and keep myself high for life? For the same reason I gave before. I couldn't summon it. It was random, and when it did manifest itself, it rarely gave me anything that could be useful in the moment. So, incredible as it may seem, I forgot about it.

Until the night I decided I had served my sentence on this earth, and it was time to be done with it all. The night I met Calvin. But what I saw in him changed everything. It was true confirmation of other realms and the wonder of the unknown, and it instilled in me a reason to delay the end, for a little while at least.

Because Calvin wasn't even real. Not that version of him, anyway.

9

"Picture your mother," I told him. "Really picture your clearest memory of her and tell me what you see."

"Why?"

"Just do it."

"It's the one I told you about. Her in bed, dying. Me trying to paint her."

"What was her name?"

"Eloise."

"Her last name?"

"I—"

"You don't remember it?"

"No."

"If I gave you a week, or a month, you still wouldn't recall it because you never knew it. What about your father?"

"What about him?"

"Do you remember him?"

"Vaguely."

"Can you picture his face?"

"No, why are you asking me all these questions?"

"The reason you say you can walk through paintings is because you came from one of them. I knew it when I saw you at the bridge, because I saw the bridge before, in a painting. It was called "End of Night" by Eloise Brunner. It depicts a haunted figure tossing scraps of paper into the river. I looked it up when we were at the library, and all the others she did. Among them is the self-portrait she painted when she had terminal cancer. She painted a figure at the foot of the bed of the son she'd lost in Afghanistan. His name was Calvin. He's depicted as the artist in the painting. It's called "The Release." I don't understand the how or the why of it no more than I understand it of my own ability, but I see you, Calvin. Just like she did. I see you, only you're just a figure from her painting. You're not the son she lost. You're fragments, a fractured, malformed thing, crammed full of confused emotions and the yearning of a dying mother."

He was silent but for the drip-drip-dripping of paint from his hands.

"You are all the sketches that didn't work. You mother painted this version of you into life. Until then, you didn't exist, and when she died, she left you behind, unable to function, an unfinished thing driven half-mad by the need to be complete."

He might have shaken his head, or perhaps it was neon's dance with the dark.

"Do you know why we're together, what attracted you to me on that bridge the night we went there to die? It wasn't just our common goal; it was that *you* saw in *me* what I am. I'm like you. I've seen the inner workings of things invisible to most. Unlike you, I can't step inside art, but I can see inside you, Calvin, and there are so many colors desperate to get out. You tried to paint them out, but that's not your destiny. That's not why you want to die. You want to open yourself up and let the paint run free, because you are the art, and you will forever suffer until you let yourself become it."

He didn't argue because I wasn't telling him anything he didn't already, on some level, know to be true. I watched him weep and the tears were thin rivers of sky-blue paint.

I wanted to touch him, to comfort him a little, but it was not yet time. "Do you trust me?"

"I don't know."

"Can you?"

He nodded.

"I love you, Calvin. I love everything that you are and are not. I love your innocence and your grief. I love your confusion, your soul, and yes, I believe you have one. I love that you're lost and alone and unknown. I love that you're here and must leave. I love that I got to taste and feel and fuck and love you. I love that I got to see you and be seen by you."

"It was the only thing that was real," he said, and when he smiled, his mouth began to run until the lower half of his face looked like a puddle of petroleum.

"Your memories: the boardwalk, your parents, the bridge. She painted a life for you and all those paintings hang in homes and galleries around the world. Everything you remember is preserved and endless. You will live on through those, so this is not an ending, because art, and therefore you, cannot die, no matter what. I will see you again."

Gently, I put a hand to his cheek. It caved beneath my touch, and I closed my eyes as, with the softest of sighs, he collapsed in a waterfall of color to the floor.

I did not open them again until I had walked to the door. There, I looked up at the painting of the barn.

It was much the same as before, only he had darkened the sky, and a figure, one must assume was himself, was standing in the door to the barn, one hand raised in greeting.

10

I drank myself into a coma, and once it passed and I could walk and the manager was hammering at the door, I showered and dressed and took a cab home. I don't like it here.

In the brief time I knew Calvin, I never invited him to my house. Part of that is good sense. Until I knew his true nature (as much as one ever can), I preferred to go on his journey with him and not fully invite him into mine. Another reason is that there are things the adventurous might uncover that I am not yet ready to explain. Things like the human eyeball in Lucite atop my nightstand, taken from the man who bit my arm and tasted oil, and the gilt-framed paintings in my living room, most of which show what you know about me thus far, the memories I shared with Calvin, and with you, whomever you may be, assuming you betrayed your true nature by standing still long enough to really look at what's been there to see all along.

My life is on that wall, and I don't know how to return to it.

My sister is there, reflected in the TV.

My father is crying in his office.

My mother is baring her teeth, clenching a fistful of hair.

Within these frames are the characters from my life.

All except the last one, which shows a bloodied patch of wallpaper and the shadow of a girl who is no longer there to cast it.

THE BINDING

Bill Cates awoke restrained. Muscles aching, he allowed himself a moment to let the panic surge unbridled through him and the hair on his neck to prickle with cold fear before he forced some measure of calm into his muscles and relaxed enough to take in his situation.

Feet and wrists bound, he winced at the starbursts of pain at the base of his neck where the skin felt like stretched leather.

He tried to move his neck but couldn't, felt resistance.

When had she bound him?

The panic ignited again but he choked it down. If she had bound him this tightly then she couldn't have gone far, wouldn't have left him in such a dangerous state where at any moment he could pass out from the lack of blood circulating to his brain. Because now he was sure she had cinched a rope around his throat too, not tight enough to strangle him, but enough so that his head sat atop the loops of cord as if severed. He could feel the coarse material biting into his flesh, his Adam's apple like an immobile rock, so that it hurt to swallow.

He could only move his eyes, and even that was a chore.

They felt dry, as if there was no air in the room. With difficulty, he used his limited view to take in the room in which she'd made him captive. All he could see were her paintings hung on the wall before him, those strange depictions of tortured creatures, all in various stages of transformation, all displayed in vibrant living color. Recollection told him that if he were able to turn around, he'd see the same ghoulish art adorning the other walls too. It was an art gallery in here.

Of course it is, she'd told him. *Art is all that means anything. All that should mean anything.*

He looked straight ahead. Something was different. Something that hadn't been there the night before. He didn't remember much but he remembered the darkness, no light filtering through from anywhere. But there was light there now, a space between the paintings.

A window.

Impossible.

And yet it *was* possible because he was looking at it—a small square window looking out onto a gleaming sunlit hallway better suited to a college or government building and not a crumbling tenement in...well, wherever *here* was. At the far end of that improbable hallway, a set of glass double doors filtered the sunlight onto the tiled floor. A ground floor.

Why would someone put a window at the end of a hallway?

No. That wasn't right. He'd been drunk, but not enough to forget the long walk up those seemingly endless flights of steps. Her apartment was on the top floor. He remembered because he'd been out of breath and sweating through his shirt by the time they'd reached her door. Why then was he now looking through a window that showed a hallway leading to doors that in turn led out onto what appeared to be a ground floor courtyard?

Then, a sound that stopped his bewilderment mid-mutter. He listened. *Voices.* He tried in vain to cock his head but was forced to strain his ears toward the sound instead.

Yes, definitely voices, but from where he couldn't tell. He couldn't see anyone through that window. Maybe it was coming from the hall? Had she returned to free him? He tried to move and the ropes bit deeper into his wrists and ankles, cinching tighter around his neck. He gave a strangled grunt of frustration. He hoped the binding wouldn't leave marks. His wife would notice the marks.

The thought of Susan finding out about any of this sent a cold lance of fear through the heat of his growing anger. She was an innocent in all of this and shouldn't have to be punished for his compulsions. Nor was she a fool. Even if he managed to persuade her the rope marks were the result of some knuckleheaded frivolity with Bill and the boys, she'd see the truth in his eyes. He'd always thought himself a good liar, until he met her and realized she was a student of men's deception, having lived a life confronted by it at every turn. Worse, she wouldn't yell, wouldn't scream, wouldn't hit him. She'd simply give him that frail, tragic smile and leave him, and the thought of being without her, a woman he truly loved despite the void inside him that led him to do foolish things, was more suffocating and torturous than the reality into which he had awakened.

Afraid now, he struggled again, and again the ropes

tightened with an awful creak.

Goddamn it. Where the hell is she?

Tired of the game, he tried to close his eyes and his heart lurched.

I can't close my eyes.

Any last vestige of calm abandoned him. He tried to open his mouth to cry out for help, to appeal to the owner of that distant mumbling voice that he was being kept prisoner here.

His mouth wouldn't open.

Oh God.

How was this possible? Had she injected him with something?

Remember her. Start by remembering her, he thought, his mind spinning so fast he was almost able to convince himself it was really his body circling the room, mercifully freed from the vicious constraints.

She drugged me. She put something in my drink.

Yes, that was it. Had to be. What other rational explanation was there? He was paralyzed, unable to move anything but his eyes. But then, why bind him?

To give the drug time to do its work.

A bar. He'd been in a bar after a meeting with Costigan's insurance people. One of their workers was threatening to sue after a routine check showed shadows on his lungs. It was a potentially disastrous situation and Bill had been drafted in to ameliorate the situation, to offer a significant amount of money to keep everybody happy and more importantly, keep it out of court and the news.

The meeting had gone well, though afterward he wasn't

entirely convinced that they were going to escape the guillotine. Still, he'd done his part and done it well and when the blonde woman at the bar started giving him the eye, he decided he had earned the reward.

Fresh anger bloomed in his chest, his hands begging to clench but frozen, a denial that further inflamed him.

That goddamn bitch. A setup. Had to be.

Red rage poured into his eyes and suddenly the urge to blink it away became a need and the need became desperation. And that led to torture as the inability to close his eyes made him want to scream, something else he couldn't do.

She had brought him back to her apartment, whispering of acts he was sure his wife had never even heard of. After the grueling ascent to her place (she told him the elevator was broken), she had led him inside. Told him to take a seat. This is where memory failed him.

Now he prayed to God to stop the madness and felt an itch wind its way like an army of fire ants over his wrists. He tried and failed to grit his teeth, to move his eyes, to adjust his position on the hard wooden chair, such automatic impulses imbued with horror by his inability to do them. Oh, to just be able to scream. Finally, aflame with agony, he looked in the only direction in which he was permitted, straight ahead through the small window and the shimmering hallway, looking less impossible now and more like the path to salvation, held cruelly out of reach for men who awoke to find themselves bound and frozen.

Oh Jesus.

Someone swept into the doorway. He paused and watched,

feeling sweat inside his skin looking for an exit that somehow wasn't there.

It was a woman, wearing an ankle-length black coat, her auburn hair dancing in the breeze before the door hissed shut behind her and let it drop to her shoulders. As she strode purposefully down the corridor, a plastic name badge flashed in the sunlight, the light hitting him straight in the eyes. His mind compensated for his mouth's uselessness and shrieked, echoing hollowly through the canals that were his nerves, setting his soul ablaze and wracking his body with shudders that rippled through his innards.

Inside, he wept, knowing no tears were spilling from his eyes because that would have taken away the burning and it was obvious to him now that no reprieve was forthcoming.

She'd left him here to die or go mad. Or both. Punishment perhaps for some crime he'd committed against someone she loved, or maybe against the marital violation he'd enlisted her help in committing against his own wife.

The woman in the hallway was coming right towards him. Surely she'd see him through the window if she came close enough? Surely she'd sound the alarm and he'd be free, weak with relief and determined to be a better man.

He listened to the clip-clop of her high heels on the tile, imagined her peering in at him and gasping, running to fetch someone to break the window, or to kick in the door of the apartment. The thought of freedom made him want to sob, if only he could.

The woman drew nearer the window and now he saw how tall she was.

She'll see me, he thought, allowing rays of his own personal sunshine to chase the shadows off his brain. *She'll call someone and they'll get me out of this goddamn chair. I'll be in pain for days, but anything will be better than...*

The woman was so close now he could see how wrong he'd been in assuming she was tall.

She wasn't tall, she was enormous and growing bigger the closer to the window she came. All hope collapsed under the sheer weight of horror.

Her face filled the window.

Or rather, her eyes did.

He felt like a bug, someone in the front row of the theater, a doll in a dollhouse, an insect, impossibly small in a world of giants. Easy prey.

His whole being erupted in a trembling panic but never moved. Couldn't move. Everything he was faltered in the face of what must surely be a god or a giant or a product of incredible trickery. It made a mockery of his hope, an idiot of his sanity.

The face moved back from the window, the expression on the woman's face one of disgust.

"This painting..." she said, her voice like thunder, sending pulses of sound vibrating through his body, "It's hideous. Why would anyone want to hang such a thing on the wall of a public building? If this is what passes for art these days, it's no wonder the world has gone to hell."

Another voice, another giant chuckled. It felt like hands clapping against his ears. His guts roiled.

Who are these...things?

"Really? I thought a painting of a bound man would have appealed to you, Detective Chambers," roared this new voice.

Detective? A picture? What are they talking about?

"Very droll, Carl. You have breakfast yet?"

"Not unless you count coffee. I've been down to Flaherty's Tavern on Third. The barman says he remembers the guy leaving with a blonde-haired woman. Couldn't remember her face though. Only the guy. He was blitzed."

Bill's brain pulsed with agony, ears near-bursting as the glass rattled between him and the giants.

No, they're not giants. It's a television screen. I'm watching a television screen she set up to confuse me. All part of whatever sick game she's playing.

The room began to vibrate again as the man continued. "The woman's clothes were spotted with paint. Barman says she wore some odd symbols around her neck too, one like a crooked pentagram, the other of a bound man. He can't swear on any of it though. Said he's not the kind of guy likes to study people."

They both looked in at Bill, who summoned the last vestiges of strength from where they had pooled somewhere in the depths of his pain-ravaged body and tried again to scream. Silence filled his throat, sweeping aside the tears, ushering them away to wherever his voice had gone and in the end he could only sit still. Numb and motionless. Watching.

The floor continued to hum.

"Like this guy."

"Yeah."

"Looks like he wants to scream."

"Gives me the creeps."

"I guess. See how the eyes follow you around the room?"

"Yeah. Like those pictures of Jesus."

He watched them, waited to wake up. Waited for salvation he had no choice but to believe would come, whether by kind or cruel means.

"I kind of like it," the man said, and moved away from the window.

No, Bill realized at last.

Not a window.

A painting.

"And I'm not even all that into art."

The woman took one last look in at Bill, looked right into his imploring eyes, and shook her head.

"This isn't art, Carl. It's punishment."

Then she too was gone, leaving Bill trapped and screaming in silence inside the frame.

PORTRAIT

"I found I could say things with color and shapes that I couldn't say any other way—things I had no words for." - Georgia O'Keeffe

It was the winter of her eighth year. The girl stood facing the window in the living room, using her index finger to draw birds in the condensation. So far there were seven of them, each one a small M with rounded shoulders, like seagulls seen from a distance. Breath pluming in the cold, she had scratched one half of the eighth M in a small patch of ice that had formed near the edge of one of the panes when something smacked into the glass on the other side. She did not scream, though the thought was there. She had gone through too much in recent months to be so affected by unanticipated events. Instead, she backed away, her young face furrowed in consternation, the small traces of ice melting beneath her fingernail, and looked toward the door, where she had expected to see her father more than an hour before. She was now late for school, but as this had become a common occurrence over the past few weeks, and as it was school after all, she wasn't very worried. She just would have liked for him to be there so she could ask him what had made the sound. But then, so often had she wished he were there, and so rarely did she see him, that she had begun to wonder if he existed at all anymore, or if, like the flurries of snow that whirled by the window, the sadness had simply swept him out of her life.

Indecision kept her in place for a few moments. She was cold. Her father usually had a fire lit by now, but, like cooking her breakfast and taking her to school, it had become another neglected duty in an ever-increasing list. She worried that he was sick, that maybe like the house, with its peeling wallpaper and cracked wainscoting, he was slowly coming apart in the wake of her mother's passing. It was a thought that filled her with dread. She couldn't lose him too. What would become of her without someone to look after her? She had no relatives that she knew of. Her only remaining grandfather had passed away the winter before. She would be well and truly alone, though in truth, even at such a young age she already knew what abandonment felt like.

One day in the fall, her mother had gone down into the basement. This was nothing new. Her studio was down there. Sometimes she stayed there for days on end. This time, however, she was down there for weeks, until Father went down to retrieve her. The girl had rounded the curve of the stairs just in time to see him dragging her mother into the hall by her ankles. She wasn't moving.

One look at her face and the girl knew why.

She was blue, her eyes the color of rubies. Her tongue was black and poking from the side of her colorless lips as if she had died making a joke. There were odd marks on her neck, like snakes made of ash. The girl stood frozen upon the stair until her father looked up and roared at her to go to her room. His eyes were red too. She could tell he'd been crying. This scared her more than anything, more than the sight of her lifeless mother being hauled like a bag of coal out of the basement, so she had done as he'd demanded and retreated to her room.

Once, she had been able to depend on her dolls for solace, but that day she saw no comfort in their faces. She saw nothing at all in their idiot stares. Worse, the pallor of their skin and the lifelessness of their glass eyes only reminded her of her dead mother. She realized henceforth they would never be able to comfort her again, and as she gathered them up one by one and stowed them in the darkness beneath her bed, where they would stay until the house collapsed in on itself three winters hence, she felt the onset of an awful kind of maturity, the death of magic and of innocence. Her toys, her only friends, often her only company, were now nothing but empty shells, childish distractions from the agony that had been waiting all along to strip her contentment away.

She never saw her mother again, though she knew where she was buried, had watched from behind her bedroom curtain as her father dug a deep hole in the back forty and tumbled the body in as if it was nothing but the carcass of some animal they had found on the road. The girl could tell from his movements that he was angry. He shoveled dirt into the hole as if he was feeding it and feared if he dawdled, it might eat him instead.

Afterward he made dinner and stared at the bowl of rabbit stew as if it was the only place left in the world to find answers, a cauldron of knowledge, and when she excused herself, he did not acknowledge her departure. He simply brought another spoonful of stew to his mouth and *slurped.* He had dolls eyes too.

Since then, she had moved like a ghost through the house, running her fingertips along the cracked walls and gathering dust from the windowsills with her fingertips. She drew pictures in her room and grew angry when they didn't turn out right. Where once she had prided herself on the straightness of her lines and the accuracy of her depictions, now she saw only ugly, melted renditions of unfamiliar things. She tried to read books—her abridged and illustrated versions of *Treasure Island* and *Heidi* and *The Count of Monte Cristo*—but the words seemed to spasm across the page like addled ants. The crosshatched illustrations perturbed her. They seemed to thrum like the struck strings of a violin. When she tried humming to herself just to have a sound other than the quiet or the intermittent settling of the house, it sounded alien to her ears, so she seldom did it for long.

The object smacking against the glass had not frightened her, but it had brought her back to herself in a way she hadn't felt since seeing her mother's body rolling over at the behest of her father's boot and tumbling down into the earth and out of her life forever. Now, she made her way into the hallway, careful not to look at the basement door, and called out for her father.

There was no answer.

She called for him again, and only the house responded, with creaks and groans and the occasional sneaky shuffle of snow sliding off the eaves. Every window was clouded by the cold, muting the light. Already her birds were fading. It made her uncomfortable, made her feel trapped, in danger of being erased too, as if the house was slowly becoming the hole in which her mother lay. Perhaps this was how ghosts were made: her mother buried, her father gone, and the girl left wandering the house until she too faded into the walls. People might wonder what had become of this once happy family, but nobody would ever find them, and soon they would be forgotten.

Weakened by hunger, she tightened her woolen coat about her, and tugged her hat down just below her eyebrows. The plan, such as it was, was simple: find her father and get him to take her to school. Ordinarily she resisted being sent to that terrible place, with its strict, sallow-faced teachers and shadow-choked rooms, where the other children looked at her with unkind eyes, and the walls were speckled with mildew, but it was the only place left where she could be free of this place. Gladly would she endure the smell of chalk dust and disinfectant, and the taunts and jeers of people she had once hoped could be her friends, if it only meant escape, even for just a little while.

Stomach rumbling, she hurried to the front of the house, where she saw that her father's boots were not in their usual place by the door, nor were the floorboards wet with melted snow, which meant he had gone outside but had yet to return.

She opened the door. The morning sun against the snow made a blazing white void of the doorway. Mittened hand shielding her eyes against the blinding glare, she cried out "Daddy?" and listened to her voice become a parody of itself as it shuddered across the fields and died in the trees at the far edge of their land. She stepped through the door and out into the cold, blinking to adjust her vision.

Slowly, the world came into focus.

Before her, a short stretch of snow-covered yard led to the barbed wire fence her father had erected around the fields. It has stood there since before she was born and a lack of maintenance over the past few years had left it looking like a sagging clothesline. The wire was rusted now, the wooden posts leaning this way and that like drunken revelers. There were snatches of sheep's hair snagged on the barbs, though the animals to which they might have belonged were long gone. It did not present much of an obstacle to the girl. She stepped gingerly over the flaccid wire, leaving it vibrating behind her, and into the field, her boots plunging into the bank of snow on the other side.

Around the field, ranks of chestnut and walnut trees stood like sketches of black lightning against the pale white sky, the frenzied reach of their mangled arms seeming to suggest a desperate desire to close the distance between them. Otherwise, the day was featureless, the landscape monochrome but for two distinctive figures, dark against the white. With no small measure of relief, and even though they were some distance away, she recognized the one on the left as her father, purely because he was ambulatory. The one on the right was the scarecrow, a humanoid formation of old clothes and branches with a gourd for a face and desiccated boots for hands and feet. She had helped her father erect the scarecrow back when he loved her and the sun still rose on their lives, back when mother would have watched them from the window above the sink with a small smile on her face. Back when the color was not restricted to her mother's paintings.

Before.

Shaking off the memory for fear the melancholy would drain her resolve and send her running back to the house and the fragile safety of her room, she trudged onward through the snow, following the clouds of her breath toward where her father was laboring over the scarecrow. Why he chose such a hostile day to attend to something that had ceased being useful a long time ago—the crows not only ignored the scarecrow, they often used its shoulders as a perch—was a mystery to her, but it hardly mattered. She was just relieved that he was there to be seen at all, because it was no longer a guarantee.

Cheeks red, teeth chattering, she navigated the snowdrifts with difficulty. It seemed to take half the day before she finally reached him. After pausing to catch her breath, the words she had rehearsed along the way bubbling into her throat, she saw something so curious, so odd and unexpected, that it killed her desire to say anything at all.

Father was there, dressed in dungarees. He wasn't wearing his coat, only a checkered shirt with the sleeves rolled up, exposing the curly ginger hair on his forearms. He did not, however, appear to be cold. Perhaps his labors kept him warm. At his feet was a large pile of letters, old by the look of them, the once-white envelopes faded to a dark yellow. Each one bore his name in block letters, but the address was not familiar. He had his back to her, unaware of her presence, and as she watched, he retrieved handfuls of those letters and stuffed them violently into the gaping chest cavity of the scarecrow, which before today had been stuffed with old clothes. Now those clothes lay in a pile at its feet.

But this was not the strangest thing. Oh, how she wished that it were.

How she now wished she hadn't left the house at all, because the scarecrow's face was no longer the smooth featureless surface of an old gourd.

It was her mother's face.

Her father had nailed a black and white portrait to it—the one that had, up until today been hanging in the upstairs hall—so that now the girl found herself being regarded by a more youthful and vibrant rendition of the woman who lay buried somewhere beneath their feet.

"Daddy?"

He had just reached down to scoop up more letters. Now he stopped, mid-stoop, and looked back over his shoulder at her. For the longest time he said nothing, just watched her with the one cold blue eye she could see. Then he straightened and turned around to face her, allowing her to see the bloody hole where his other eye should have been. The cheek beneath it was streaked with snow-flecked gore and blood, and now the girl had to back away in horror, one hand over her mouth, her body wracked with shivers she could no longer blame on the cold.

"Sweetheart," her father said, and when he opened his mouth, she could see that some of his teeth were missing too. "I'm so glad you're here."

Behind him, she registered what might be the oddest thing of all. Propped up in a heap of snow was something she had missed from a distance because it had blended in with the colorlessness of the day. Now that she could see it, she felt a curious mixture of emotions because although it didn't belong out here in the field, not now, not today, it was something she had desperately wanted for as long as she could recall.

"I got you a birthday present," her father said, his face spread in a smile she didn't care for at all.

It wasn't her birthday. Hadn't been for months, but she remembered the disappointment upon waking that day to find that, not only had she not gotten what she'd asked for, she'd gotten nothing at all, and the house was silent. No gifts, no celebrations, no cake, just her parents shut away in separate rooms and the girl left to pout all alone until she forced the dolls to join her in an impromptu and pitiful tea party.

"Do you like it?"

She had asked her parents for an easel and some paints. Watercolors would do if oils were too expensive, she'd told them. She wasn't fussy. She knew money was tight and really, she just wanted to make pictures on something other than another of her mother's raggedy old sketch pads. Her father had seemed ambivalent, her mother horrified, then angry, a reaction the girl didn't understand. She thought her mother would be proud that her daughter wanted to follow in her footsteps and become an artist.

Instead, her mother locked herself in the basement, which doubled as her studio, and tore the place apart.

But now here it was, the very thing she'd asked for, in the last place she expected to see it.

"Daddy..." She didn't know what to say. Part of her desperately wanted to appreciate the acquisition of the long-desired gift, but all of this felt so very wrong. What had happened to her father? Who or what had hurt him and why was he not hurrying to the hospital? And the letters...and the picture of her mother nailed to the scarecrow's face...it all felt like a nightmare. Only the biting cold told her that it wasn't.

"I'm sorry," her father said, and his face fell, his one remaining eye watering. "I forgot to get the paints. My head was hurting so bad. I was home before I remembered them."

Between the half-sunken wooden legs of the easel, she saw what might have been the handle of a shovel. She watched as her father walked to the easel, stepped behind it, and retrieved the object.

"But I have a way to fix that for you, honey."

It was not a shovel, after all, but his hunting rifle.

"What are you doing?" Her voice sounded brittle, as if it had become ice melting on her tongue.

He walked slowly toward her, the sadness still on his face though he was still smiling. Spots of blood marked his passage. He almost lost his footing as he approached where she stood paralyzed by fear.

"What she told me to do," he said and stopped between the girl and the easel.

"Daddy, please, I'm scared."

When he smiled, she saw that his lips were grey and trembling, his gums raw and bleeding.

"Don't be. I have something else for you too. Would you like it?"

She shook her head and backed another step away from him.

"There's nothing to be afraid of. All of this is the start of something wonderful. It's freedom."

Again, she shook her head. “Please, let’s just go back to the house. We can light a fire and make some food, or...or...”

“Sweetheart, listen to me. I know I haven’t been myself. I know I haven’t been okay. But I’m going to make that up to you now, okay?”

A flock of ravens exploded from the trees to her right, but she paid them no mind. Couldn’t have diverted her attention from her father’s face even if she’d wanted to. It had become her whole world.

“How?” she asked him, despite her terror. All she wanted was for everything to go back to the way it was before.

Still sad, still smiling, he reached into the pocket of his dungarees and produced a small stubby red pencil, no bigger than her pinky. He held it out, ice crystals sparkling in the edges of his hollow eyesocket as the blood began to freeze.

“I want you to take this.”

“Why?”

“I want you to take this and I want you to go over and write your name in the lower right-hand corner of that canvas.”

“I don’t want to.” She was sobbing now. Her head hurt from the force of the tears and she tasted salt on her tongue. Her legs were shaking so bad she was not sure how long more they’d keep her upright. “Please, let’s just go home.”

“Write your name like I asked you to and we can be done. But you must do it. Your mother said so.”

“Why?”

“Because it’s how you start over.”

“I don’t know what that means.”

"You will, but you have to do what you're told. If you don't, nothing changes. And even worse, you'll be disrespecting your mother's wishes." Absently, he reached up a hand and scratched with a forefinger at the edges of the raw red hollow in his face. It bled anew. "And even though she's dead, she'll know, and that will be the worst thing of all."

The cold had crept inside her coat, inside her skin. She was powerless to keep from shaking. "W-why did sh-she die?" It was the question she had wanted to ask, a truth she needed to understand, ever since the day she'd watched him drag her mother out of the basement. She'd known, even if she hadn't fully comprehended how such a thing could happen, or why, that her mother wasn't well in the mind. In the weeks, perhaps months leading up to her death, she had changed, become a frightening shadow of herself. She had faded, yes, that was the word, as if someone or something had been slowly draining her of color. Now, her father looked the same.

"She died because she needed to," he said.

"Why did she need to?"

"Because she knew it was the right thing, the only thing to do if there was to be any hope of saving you."

The girl was confused and frightened and thus the tears came freely. She expected her father to take her in his arms, to hold her until the worst of the pain went away, to tell her, like he used to, that he was her special girl, that he would never let anything hurt her. But that's not what he did. Instead, he dropped to his haunches, wincing involuntarily at some unknown discomfort in his knee, and he looked squarely at her, one hand braced in the snow to steady himself, the other around the unbreeched stock of the rifle. He held the pencil out to her.

"Go write your name where I told you to."

Again, she wanted to ask why. None of this made any sense. She desperately wanted to defy him, to turn and run, maybe keep running until she reached the school. There perhaps she could find someone who would listen, and help. Maybe they would send an ambulance out to the farm and they could fix her father's eye and whatever else was wrong with him. Maybe the situation could still be salvaged before she lost everything.

But what if they took him away and he never came back? What then?

Again, she looked up at the scarecrow. The tears in her eyes made it appear to move and rendered her mother's smiling face a gray smudge beneath a windblown puddle.

"It was what she wanted for you."

As much as she loved her father, it was getting harder to meet what remained of his gaze, so she took the pencil, stepped around him, and walked the few short feet to where the easel stood waiting. Down in the lower right-hand corner of the easel, she wrote her name in cursive, the tip of her tongue protruding from the side of her mouth as a force of habit. At school she had been working on making her letters more like her mother's, but while there was certainly a touch of floridity to it, it still lacked the elegance of her mother's signature. Once done, she stepped back from the canvas. She was chilled to the bone now and couldn't help wondering how long she was going to be out here. There was no fire at home. If she pacified her father, would he come home and help her warm the house, perhaps make them something to eat? That the pantry was bare of food mattered little. It was his duty to provide.

But would he? And what was she to do if he didn't?

"Take the canvas down," he instructed.

She didn't ask why. It didn't matter anymore. She just had to do as she was told until she could figure out a better course of action. Fleeing was the dominant impulse, but she knew she wouldn't get far through the deep snow before he caught up to her.

She reached up and grabbed the edges of the large canvas and gingerly removed it from the easel. It was heavier than she'd expected and she almost went sprawling, but she redoubled her efforts, spreading her feet to compensate for the weight, and took a step backward.

But for her signature, the canvas was blank, the unblemished white making it seem as if she had signed her name on a piece of the winter sky.

"What should I do with it?" she asked.

"Kneel down and hold it in front of you as if it's a mirror."

"Why?"

"Because it soon will be."

She heard rustling behind her and, filled with the sudden and terrifying feeling that he was about to force his request upon her, she dropped down on her knees into the snow, the canvas propped up before her.

"Good girl."

"What do I do now?"

An eternity of cold confusion passed before he replied, long enough for her to start to worry that maybe he had just gone away and left her here alone.

"You become."

"Become what?"

She heard a sound that was both familiar and horrible: the ratcheting click of the hammer being drawn back on the hunting rifle. Instantly she was paralyzed, her eyes widening, throat dry, the shakes intensifying. She felt her bladder let go and wet warmth spreading across her groin and down over her legs. The heat was merciful only for a moment before it quickly began to cool.

No matter her confusion and fear thus far, the only possibility she hadn't considered was that her father might want to hurt her, or worse.

"Daddy?" She didn't want to turn around, but desperately needed to, if only to assure herself that her father wasn't standing there pointing the rifle at her. Unable to bear it any longer, she risked a quick glance.

Her father was still kneeling in the snow and facing away from her just like she'd left him. She couldn't see the rifle.

"Look at the canvas, sweetheart," he said.

"What are you doing? Why are we out here?"

"Look at the canvas, honey."

"Daddy, please."

"Look at what's there to be seen."

Terrified to the core of her being, but equally afraid to disobey him, she could only do as he'd asked. Jolted by wave after wave of tears and shivering so bad her muscles ached, she looked at the canvas held in her hands, at the endless expanse of white blending in with the field and sky behind it and waited.

Enough time passed that she felt the wetness in her pants start to freeze.

Enough time for her to run out of tears and for darkness to begin to edge its way like spilled ink between the trees.

Enough time for her to reach a place where she now just wanted to sleep.

Then her father said, in little more than a whisper, "I love you, Beth," and she was instantly awake.

She looked up at the precise moment he pulled the trigger. The roar of thunder was so loud it might have come from inside her. She flinched, screaming as wet spray soaked her hair and carried on, drenching the canvas before her.

All except the outline of her head and shoulders, now the only negative space in a dripping crimson picture.

She stared at the white portrait of herself amid the red until her muscles went numb, until sirens filled the air, until the light started to leave the sky and strangers beseeched her to rise.

Her father had told the truth. This was the start of something, at her mother's bequest. It was a gift. She could feel it, a small cold fire in the pit of her stomach, though she didn't yet know its full nature. But she knew she would never speak again, not in words anyone would understand, the same way the sheer power of the need to create had silenced her mother. She would have to paint her story for them and hope that made more sense.

Before they forced her to stand, she secreted the pencil in her pocket, her mind already filled with images she yearned to bring to life, every one of them red.

THE ACQUISITION

Carnegie Hill, New York

Though the day had been long and less than remarkable, from the unexpected wait for his usual table at Le Paris, to the news that his friend Bill Glass's cancer had returned, Julius was nevertheless unable to contain his excitement as he mounted the steps to his townhouse. Ill-tidings aside—and really, if Bill had beaten that foul disease once, there was nothing to suggest he couldn't again; the old man was strong as an ox—this was a day he had been anticipating for weeks, ever since he had received the certificate of authenticity from his man in Manhattan for the Verner piece. That he'd managed to find anyone to authenticate the painting at all was nothing short of a miracle. Once upon a time, he could have had one of the good folks at the Warhol or Noguchi take a peek, but these days fear of litigation from swindled collectors had led even the most qualified experts in the business to strike that particular talent from their resumes. It was an alarming development. Should the day come in which authenticators vanished completely, it would throw the art world into turmoil. Fakes and forgeries would abound and if one could no longer trust in the purity of the water, where would the incentive be to continue drinking from the well? It was a disturbing thought, and one Julius was not eager to dwell upon. Besides, art had endured worse challenges. Opposing ideologies had rid France of wide swaths of art during the Revolution. Cubism and surrealism had burned in the flames of Hitler's purge on "degenerate art". George Washington's trek across the Delaware had been halted by air raids during World War II, and there had been countless attempts to disfigure the Mona Lisa. Still, art prevailed because mankind simply could not live without it. Just as creation begets destruction, so too does destruction beget creation.

The old man smiled as he fished his keys from his pocket and opened the front door. He would have to remember that line at MOMA's next fundraiser.

His hands were shaking with anticipation as he hurried inside and shut the outer door on the late evening chill. A pause to consider his reflection in the beveled glass showed a much younger man, rid of the myriad lines and pouches beneath the eyes. Julius nodded his approval. Enthusiasm was a wonderful thing, and nothing enthused him more than the acquisition of a rare work of art. But as he shrugged out of his overcoat, kicked off his shoes and slipped his stockinged feet into the monogrammed slippers Elsa had dutifully left for him by the door, he realized *rare* wasn't the right word at all. The Verner piece was beyond rare, because up until a week ago, nobody even knew it existed. And while he didn't consider himself a greedy man—snide intimations from those hacks in the *Times* aside—it did rather gall him that there were sixteen more pieces out there he would probably never get to see in person, especially if they ended up in private collections, or worse, galleries abroad. No matter what the mirror told him, he was too old to travel like he had back in the day, one of the many realities of age that made his heart ache. Besides, seeing them would only inflame his need to possess them, and he suspected he was lucky he had managed to acquire one at all. In every respect, provenance had delivered it to his door.

"Elsa?"

The house was quiet but for the clucking of the grandfather clock in the hall. He waited a few moments for his housekeeper to appear. When she didn't, he waved a wrinkled hand in the direction of her memory and shuffled off to the living room to fetch his own drink. It was not an evening in which he was content to wait to be attended to, nor did he feel like wasting time hunting her down. She could be chastised in the morning.

In the living room, he was glad to see that the men he had tasked to deliver the painting had, as per his instructions, already unpacked it for him. Ideally, he would have preferred to have been present to oversee its arrival and unboxing for fear the men did not exercise enough care, but alas, the unprecedented delay at Le Paris and the grim phone call from Bill had denied him the luxury. Still, better they took care of the hardest work than leave him to do it himself. His arthritis, a burden on the best days, had started gnawing at his bones with the settling of the autumnal cold, making his joints feel as withered as the leaves. The mere thought of having to pull the crate apart to get to his prize made his knuckles throb.

As he went to the corner bar to pour himself a sherry, he was struck again by a note of irritation that the ordinarily loyal Elsa was in absentia, for he could have used her hands. He supposed she might have gone home, though it was rare for her to do so before his arrival. It was also possible she had informed him of some pressing family business or prior engagement, and he had simply forgot. That seemed to happen more and more these days, his mind not being what it used to be. In such instances, he turned hostile toward the housekeeper, his caustic disposition masking his fear at the steady decline of his faculties. She was no fool, of course. He sometimes suspected she knew him better than he ever would, and thus she accepted his impromptu belligerence with maddening grace. *Yes, Mr. Julius. Will there be anything else, Mr. Julius?* And always with that withering look. The memory of it summoned a touch of a smile. Incorrigible as she was, she was also the closest he had or would ever come to a wife unless he lost his mind and decided to take some gold-digging floozy for a bride for the sake of vanity, like so many of his fellows had done.

Such things did not interest him.

He had Elsa and he had his art and that was company enough. Thus, he would never admit into his sanctum some surgery-enhanced dilettante whose very appearance flew in the face of the collection he had spent a lifetime cultivating, just so he could die and bestow upon her wealth she had not earned. Besides, he had no need of a trophy wife. All his trophies were downstairs in the climate-controlled room he called The Vault.

Although his body quaked with the need to unveil the

painting, which the delivery men had left still encased in foam and brown paper on the mahogany table in the middle of the room, Julius went instead to the large ornate fireplace and stared down into the flames, content to wring from the occasion a few more moments of suspense. After all, once the painting was unveiled and hung in its carefully selected place in The Vault, he would never be able to recapture this moment, the precious time in which he got to carefully tear away the wrapping and see it up close for the first time. The intoxication of discovery, the thrill of the unveiling, the rush of knowing he held in his hands a rare treasure nobody else could see unless he allowed them the privilege, which undoubtedly, he would, assuming they were connoisseurs, people he wished to impress. Art like this was not intended to be squandered on the uninitiated and would be valueless to ignorant eyes.

In whatever time remained to a man of his years, there would be other treasures, other paintings, each one accompanied by its own moment of intoxication, but with the Verner, as with all the others, each occasion was different in subtle ways. With this one, which the artist had titled "The Womb", the fact that its existence had only come to light a few weeks ago made it a very special acquisition indeed. Though the collection had yet to be made public, the art-world was already abuzz. If he picked up the phone and called his dealer, Julius fully expected to hear that all the remaining pieces had sold. And why not? There are few things more exciting than the revelation that a deceased creator left previously undiscovered work in their wake. The news is a salve on the wound their passing leaves behind.

He drained the sherry and carefully set the glass down on the mantel. Rubbing his hands together briskly, his face spread in a smile, he made his way to the table where the painting awaited him.

As he'd instructed, Elsa had left a pair of blue nitrile gloves on the table next to the package. He removed his jacket and laid it over the top of the wingback chair behind him, rolled up his shirt sleeves, and put on the gloves. He could get as touchy feely as he liked once he'd inspected the piece, but it wouldn't do to damage it during the unwrapping, or before he had verification that everything was in order.

Gently, he undid the tape on the front seam of the brown paper and pushed the flaps to the side. He could just about make out the dark square of the painting beneath the protective plastic sheeting. Hands trembling, palms moist beneath the gloves, he ever-so-carefully removed the plastic and set it aside. Now the picture was revealed to him, the brown paper spread out on both sides of it like the wings of a mummified bird.

The old man felt the breath rush from his lungs. Tears pricked his eyes.

It was so very easy to forget the power of Elizabeth Verner's work, and he felt a tiny stab of shame that he had been so critical of it in her heyday. If he remembered correctly, his issue was that her work had always been too derivative of the past masters. While mimicry was common, even among the greats, to Julius, there was never enough of *her* in her work to think of them as anything other than homages. While he'd acknowledged her talent, it irritated him that she seemed determined to hide herself from the viewer. Reticence in a painter's work was hardly uncommon, but where an artist like Pollock could reveal his true self on the canvas and *then* go to great lengths to obscure it, Verner's just had a vacancy where her truth should have been, an absence that forced the critical eye to pay more attention to her flaws and appropriations. That there was more honesty, more of the woman in the work toward the end of her life was the real tragedy because by then her name had already fallen out of favor. There were newer, bolder, more exciting talents, and the name Elizabeth Verner became just another footnote in New York's long history of passing fancies. The assumption was that she'd either given up painting, or simply stopped selling them. That she'd appeared only briefly to reinvent herself as some kind of feminist witch did not even bear comment, though it did make him marvel at the lengths to which people were willing to go to destroy their reputations once they realized the time had passed to recapture them. Her death, it seemed, was something of a blessing, then. Not only did the mad old woman finally find some peace, the art world saw the removal of the sole obstruction to her private works. Thank God he'd had the wherewithal to bring her work to an appraiser or they might have ended up hawked for a pittance at some yard sale.

He shuddered at the thought.

Before him on the table, was a painting few people knew much about other than the name on the list the artist's ex-husband had submitted to Julius's dealer: "The Womb."

And it was breathtaking, the kind of work of which he had always assumed the artist capable, hence his frustration at her inability to deliver it. But here it was, a surrealist portrait of darkness that made his stomach quiver and intensified the trembling in his hands. Electric with excitement and moved nearly to tears, his hands unsure where to go, he hurried back to the bar, poured himself another sherry and quickly downed it, then returned to the table, and "The Womb".

Still wearing the gloves, he reached down, grabbed the upper corners of the painting's gilded frame, and raised it upright so that it was standing on the table in front of him.

In the light, it was even more magnificent and affecting, and now the tears did come, trickling down his face. He moved back a step so they would drip to the floor and not onto the table, or worse, the art, then wiped his eyes and returned to his appraisal, a trembling hand before his face.

The painting depicted an antiquated drawing room, much like his own, but crowded with hundreds of books, all their covers red. They'd been crammed into the lofty bookshelf to the left of the frame and crowded the floor on all but one side. In the center of the picture, a white-framed window showed absolute darkness through its panes, with the faintest suggestion of the artist's reflection, though he would need a magnifying glass to confirm it was more than just a pale smudge. To the right of the frame, more shelves, more books. Under the window—and yes, that was a face in the glass, wasn't it?—was a wooden table with clawfoot legs. There were more books, none of which bore titles, stacked atop it. And in the shadows beneath the table was a pregnant woman. She was sitting naked with her back against the wall, arms to her side, legs splayed, and though her face was but a cream thumbprint unmarred by features, it was somehow clear that she was in pain. If a child had produced itself, however, any suggestion of it was lost in the dense shadow cloaking her sex.

Julius nodded his appreciation. It was a dark piece, that was for sure, but then Verner had never been known for her light, even in person. Indeed, she was better remembered as a sad creature with clear mental issues and questionable hygiene, which to be fair, only verified her as a bona fide artist in the eyes of the connoisseurs. As Bill liked to say: "Show me a sane artist and I'll show you a fraud." The smell, he would quip, was simply unfermented money.

In the coming days, Julius planned to research as much as possible about the artist's life in the hope of decoding a possible meaning from this painting. Was the figure meant to represent the agony of childbirth? Why was the woman hidden? Shame? Was the child the product of an illicit tryst? Given what he knew of Verner's politics, could it be a feminist piece? And who was the woman? A deceased mother or sister or a figure from her imagination? Was it the artist herself? Van Gogh's work had always in some way depicted his feelings of estrangement, of alienation from his father, from the world, and then, toward the end, served as a veritable road map of his insanity and impending self-destruction. His entire life, both the good and the bad, could be found in his paintings. Therein the demons lay. For Julius, part of the fun was solving the mystery behind the images. It invigorated him, made him feel like a detective. Plus, it would increase the value of the piece, if only in cachet, if he had a good tale to accompany it.

After fetching himself another sherry—he reminded

himself to be careful not to let his senses get too dull—he returned to the painting and found, after some untold amount of time, and much to his surprise, that he was laughing uncontrollably. Perhaps it was the sherry that made him feel suddenly giddy. Perhaps it was the shifting of the light—whether real or imagined—that made it seem as if the figure beneath the table in the picture had raised its head and was staring straight at him with eyes that were tiny red sparks in the black. He found this only moderately odd. The abrupt pain in his temples was worthier of note, and yet he couldn't stop the laughter from bubbling up out of him long enough to give it the proper consideration. The more he tried to stop, the worse it got, until he abandoned the idea entirely and took his hand from his mouth.

The glove came away soaked in blood.

Some small faraway part of his mind notified him that this was a matter of great concern, but he disregarded the voice and returned his attention to the painting, where quite curiously now, the woman was gone. Guffawing still, tears streaming from his eyes, he squinted and leaned in closer to the painting to see if he could divine the figure after all.

"It's fine," he told himself, despite the insistent screaming of a panicked voice deep down inside him. "It's all in order. She just moved further back into the shadows, that's all. Probably to be away from the mad old man."

At the precise moment that he realized the painting was standing upright without anything to support it, and had been for quite some time, he sensed movement beneath the table. Not the one in the painting, but his own. Blood running freely from his nose, he looked down, his belly still jiggling with mirth that refused to abate and saw the flash of a pale white arm withdrawing into the shadows, like a fish catching the sun in shallow water before returning to the deep.

"There you are," Julius said, unconsciously wiping his sleeve across his nose.

Twin sparks hovered just beneath the hem of the tablecloth, the fire reflected in a glassy stare.

"You builders of the sky made it an uneven weight," said a voice. "It presses so much harder on our shoulders."

The old man nodded at the voice, which sounded like someone speaking through the blades of a fan. "Yes," he said aloud as the tears obscuring his vision turned red. "Yes, of course we did. It was never made clear that we should care."

The room smelled like fresh paint.

"You drove us into the ground to keep us clawing for air. Why build the world at all if you'd rather we didn't see it?"

He turned and staggered toward the opposite side of the room, toward the fireplace. And although he chewed through his tongue before he had a chance to express aloud his absolute joy at having the true meaning of the painting explained, thereby saving him weeks of research, it was enough to know.

A privilege to know.

And it was so much more than he'd expected, than he'd been ready to learn.

As he dropped to his knees before the fire, Julius was glad they didn't hurt anymore. The cold weather had made them stiff as boards lately. Now, he wept with gratitude that they would never bother him again. She had promised him that, and so much else.

Thank you, Mother, he thought.

On hands and knees, the old man crawled into the fireplace, his palms crunching into the burning logs, feet kicking embers out behind him onto the carpet. He was still holding the glass in one hand, but it shattered in short order, the sherry igniting and sending a mixture of blue and red flame racing up his arm.

There, on the coals, he lay on his side, knees drawn up, head bowed, and waited in the flames.

The room began to burn and before the heat burst his eyes, he saw the artist standing before him, watching, shimmering in the heat. She appeared to be smiling, as any artist will when their work is finally understood.

THE BARBED LADY WANTS FOR NOTHING

"The hell kind of name is that for a bookstore?"

I shook my head, only because I didn't want to get into an argument with Kane about the proprietor's choice of title. He was the kind of guy that loved to lose his temper because it served as a distraction, kept him from looking too closely at the shambles his life had become.

Although I never told him as much, I could relate. In fact, I didn't know anyone who couldn't. The world had gone to hell.

Rain ran down my neck in icy streams while Kane huffed and snorted his derision up at the green neon gorgon leering at us from the sign. I nudged him into moving. "C'mon, he'll be closing soon."

Above our heads, the glowing green letters read:

THE BARBED LADY WANTS FOR NOTHING

I agreed with Kane that it was an odd name for a store but not one that specialized in rare and out-of-print science fiction novels. I remembered a time when this place had been my utopia.

The small golden bell above the door announced our arrival to the only ears inside the bookshop, those of the venerable Arthur Glimmsbury.

"Egads, a customer. No wait, two customers! Is it Christmas already?" he quipped as we both shuddered off the rain and glided toward him.

He stood behind a waist-high mahogany counter, large thick fingers splayed out atop the surface like claws, his nails polished crimson. He grinned from ear to ear, allowing us to see our harried reflections in his silver teeth. Tufts of hair curled up from his peeling pate like frozen smoke, held in place by some lubricant of which we were blissfully unfamiliar.

Kane grunted and nudged me forward. I sighed. I had known Arthur for years and though the name had changed many times since my childhood, the bookstore had always been here, always smelling of dust and age and mildewing secrets. A quaint outpost untouched by the barreling, destructive train of time.

I had never considered the old man with the ruby eyes a friend, but his face was a part of the neighborhood that had seen me grow into the fine, strapping young criminal that I became. And this most unpleasant of characteristics had brought me back to him tonight, to the bookstore with the name Kane didn't like, to rob the old man.

"So, what pleases you on this dismal evening?" Arthur said with a silvery smile and winked, his wrinkled lid making a faint sucking sound as it slid over the scarlet gem in his eye socket. At my back, Kane snickered.

The rain hissed against the pavement outside, only

slightly muted by the large plate glass windows. Kane's boots clacked against the hardwood floor in a Morse code of impatience.

"We're here for your money, Arthur. All of it."

If he'd had an eyebrow, it would have risen where the pink bulb of flesh now wrinkled in surprise. Or was it amusement?

"I see. Won't you check out my new comic line first? I managed to rescue some truly ancient copies of *Ray Gunn* and *Troll City*. There are some more recent copies of Salamander Nights too. You'll remember they sold out when that bizarre religion came over—"

"Hey, did you hear what he *said*, old man?" Kane growled, pushing me aside and slamming his tattooed knuckles down on the counter. "We didn't come here for comic books. We want the money and if you intend to see tomorrow, you'd better haul yourself to where the credits are at, capisce?"

This time it was definitely amusement peppering Glimmsbury's cheeks. "*Salamander Nights* really took off though, didn't it? Who would have thought a comic book would have had such a resounding influence on such troubled times? You really should—"

"No, *you* really should clean the wax out of your ears and do what you're told or I'm gonna have to show you a few antiques of my own," Kane said patting the bulge in his raincoat. The old man shrugged and the movement allowed me to see the sparkling light in the wall behind him. Understanding flowed over me and I tapped Kane on the shoulder.

He spun, teeth clenched. "What?"

"Look behind him."

"Yeah, what? I—" He trailed off and rage contorted his gaunt features. "He's a goddamn hologram?"

"Looks like it, but he must be projecting himself from somewhere in the store."

Kane scoffed. "No wonder he was so ballsy. Well, this is just peachy. 'Straight in, straight out' you said. I'm a bigger fool for listening to you."

"That could indeed be the case. It really does pay off to know the place you intend to rob," Glimmsbury commented. Without a word, Kane whipped out his revolver and pumped three bursts into the bejeweled Holo light in the wall. It fizzed and crackled and coughed black smoke as Glimmsbury shriveled out of existence.

We broke up and began searching the store.

While Kane made as big a mess as possible, knocking over bookshelves and overturning baskets full of cheesy paperbacks, I wandered down the aisles where I knew from past visits the old man kept the ancient comic books.

"Where the hell is he?" Kane roared. "Is there a back room?"

"Yeah, but make sure you lock the front door or we'll have vigilantes all over us before we get a chance to look." Bad enough we had the cops to contend with, now neighborhoods were amassing veritable armies to keep us from doing what we had to.

He cursed and a moment later, a lock snapped closed.

I found myself in an aisle, six shelves high on both sides and packed full of old comic books preserved like mummies in their dustproof shrouds.

Images of spacemen in laughably inept attire battling multi-headed aliens on barren dusty planets and sexy, scantily clad beauties caught in the act of shrieking as untold horrors bore down on them, filled the shelves. I smiled despite myself, remembering a childhood not always tainted by corruption and the many nights in my room reading *Ray Gunn* long after I was supposed to be sleeping. It was a warm memory that I shelved with the promise that it wouldn't stay there forever.

On the center shelf, just above eye-level were all twelve copies of *Salamander Nights.* I knew they were priceless, the dozen copies having sold out immediately on release by fans eager to escape the generic retreads being shoved in their faces in an attempt to restore commercial thinking and family values. *Salamander Nights* had been a rage, a pop phenomenon destined to fade into obscurity but not without leaving a few lives touched by the experience.

Sadly, mine hadn't been one of them.

"What the hell are you doing back there?" Kane said and I looked to my left at his scarecrow-like silhouette at the top of the aisle. "Catching up on your reading?"

"I'll be there in a minute," I said, my eyes alighting on something on the shelf nearest the floor. "Go check out the back room."

"Hey, less ordering, buddy. I don't work for you."

I shrugged. "Whatever. You want the money or not?"

He spat and stalked off muttering obscenities.

But at that moment, his attitude was lost on me. I dropped to my haunches and stared in bewilderment at the comic that had caught my attention. Water pooled around my feet as I reached out and gently picked it up.

"This isn't right," I whispered.

The comic book had a color and ink drawing of the very bookstore in which I now stood clutching the comic book on the cover. The sign above the drawing read: THE BARBED LADY WANTS FOR NOTHING, complete with lovingly rendered green neon gorgon.

The name of the comic was *Salamander Nights*: Issue #13.

"Aha! Gotcha!" Kane yelled in triumph as the sound of screeching metal reached me through the shelves. "I found a door!"

I didn't answer. Couldn't. Compelled by a curiosity long abandoned, I had opened the comic book and was now staring at another picture of the bookstore, smaller and less detailed but with no doubt as to what it represented. I felt my heart turn to cold crystal, sending shards of glass shooting into my throat.

Outside the store stood two men.

A speech bubble hung between them.

Written in small, barely legible lettering inside the bubble was: "The hell kind of name is that for a bookstore?"

The thumping continued as Kane struggled to get the door open.

I flicked through the pages, my eyes stinging with sudden panic at the barely glimpsed images populating the pages.

It was a chronicle of this night, every detail, every nuance and every ounce of dialogue captured, our story set in gloomy colors for the world to see.

Or for *me* to see.

A trick. It had to be. I ran my fingers over the pages, testing it, hoping the ink would run beneath my damp fingers. Such a simple thing could have convinced me that this was an elaborate hoax perpetrated by Glimmsbury but the moisture on my fingertips did nothing but darken the images.

I heard the metal door shriek and clatter, followed by another triumphant holler from Kane. "I got it open! You comin?"

"Just a second," I called to him, hoping the unease hadn't been evident in my voice. Kane would have a field day with any sign of weakness.

"Fine," he answered. "But I get a bigger cut for doing all the grunt work."

I turned the page and there I was, down on my haunches, brooding over a comic book. It was starting to make my head hurt.

The next panel showed Kane battering the door, teeth clenched, with his thick-soled boots leaving muddy rainwater dripping down the blue metal. He had been drawn as the villain, a stereotype, the bad guy who gets his comeuppance in the end by less than pleasant means. Five o' clock shadow shaded his comic book self's jaw, his eyes dark as night as he focused on the task at hand.

The next panel showed him grinning at the open door. A speech bubble snaked from between his yellow teeth.

"It's dark back here," the real-world Kane said and I followed his progress inside by turning the page.

I read my lines like an actor at an audition: "So find a light."

I flipped the page and terror stuck like a chicken bone in my throat. I jumped to my feet, almost slipping in the puddle that had gathered while I read. The last page.

"Oh Jesus. Kane!" I cried out, my eyes hopping from panel to panel, from one horrifying image to the next. Amid them all was Glimmsbury, red jeweled eyes sparkling in the gloom, looking like he'd always looked, smiling and patient. But this image showed something in his face I had never seen before: Malice.

"Kane!"

"What, what? The hell you screeching for?"

"Get away from the door."

"What?"

I read my lines, the dizzyingly surreal quality of the scene perfect for the comic book in my hands, but utterly horrifying outside it. "I said—" My caricature stopped in mid-sentence.

Four panels from the end. This panel devoted entirely to darkness except for the speech bubble representing Kane's sudden terror. "Hey. What's—?"

"Kane, get out of there!" I screamed, wanting to run from the store, wanting to run to help Kane but afraid of the thing the comic book told me was in there with him; refusing to believe this bundle of recycled paper could be right about anything and yet it was. I was watching it unfold.

My shadowed caricature showed my face stretched by fear. Ghostly bubbles over my head told me I could flee, that I could live with the guilt of leaving Kane to die just as I had lived with guilt all my life.

Third panel from the end.

"Oh God!" Kane screamed and I flinched at the sound even though I had known it was coming. I looked back down at the comic book, suddenly and horrifyingly aware that only a series of shelves stood between that door and me.

The shadows in the back room parted like a curtain and Kane became the wearer of that oft-used defensive pose, so popular for comics of this type.

"Kane!"

The second last panel showed a slim pair of light green arms reaching for the stricken victim from somewhere offstage, thorn-like protuberances studding its skin, black tattoos threading their way over the flesh like vines. Over where the darkness concealed its face, the artist had speckled in amber sparks to convey a multitude of hungry eyes. A cheap way of doing it, but oh so very effective now.

And I had full sound effects to accompany the pictures.

I dropped the comic. It fluttered into the puddle on the floor like a dead bird. I ran the length of the aisle and wrestled with the door, forgot the lock, remembered the lock, opened the door and burst out of the store with a scream to drown out those at my heels.

I ran, and ran, propelled by that last scene in a comic book no-one knew existed, that perhaps didn't exist except for two men who'd picked the wrong store to rob.

The last panel.

That hideous image of the store's namesake...

Not nearly so absurd looking in the flesh.

THE AMP

Transcript of *Crash Metal* Interview with Jay "The Rooster" Roswell, July 17th, 1996. Conducted by Pete Stewart

[PS] You say you were there when Erich Carey died?

[JR] Hell yeah, man. It was wild. In ways you wouldn't believe.

[PS] Can you tell me about the events leading up to that night?

[JR] It was sad, man. I mean, we all used to be tight. I've been with them since we were kids. I couldn't play music for shit. Just don't have that kinda talent, but they always wanted me around, y'know? To haul gear, go on beer runs, or whatever. Kept me out of trouble. Most of the time. [laughs] But Kerry grew up around the corner from me. We used to play stickball and shit. Real tomboy. Never took lip from anybody. I had a crush on her right up until the end. She was too into Erich, though, so I never made a move. Didn't want to piss him off. He had a temper. Like that time he tried to set fire to the bar in Sioux Falls because the crowd were assholes. Typical frontman, I guess. Nobody ever knew how much was real and how much was for show. I loved him though. And Kerry and Joss. No matter what you read about them, their antics and such, they were good people, and they were my friends. But Erich got weird in the end, as so many of them do. Though with him, it wasn't just the drugs and the alcohol and whatever else he was doing. I think a lot of the change in him came about after he found that amp.

[PS] Amp?

[JR] Yeah, man. A little grey practice thing. Vacuum tube, open cabinet, no brand name, and beat to shit. So crooked it had to be propped up because the base didn't sit right on the floor. Looked like it would fall apart if you tried to pick it up. But Erich didn't care. He showed up to rehearsal one day carrying that thing like it was a newborn baby or something. We all sat around while he set it up, wondering what he expected to get out of it.

[PS] And what did he get out of it?

[JR] Someone else's sound.

[PS] What does that mean?

[JR] I mean, he plugged it in, hooked his axe up to it, and started playing, but the song he was playing isn't what came out of that amp. It was a totally different song, unlike any I've ever heard, and it made my head hurt. Like I had hornets behind my eyes. Must've had the same effect on Kerry, because she came out from behind the drumkit and unplugged that amp with a look on her face like someone had died.

[PS] Can you describe the song?

[JR] No, and if I could, I don't think I'd want to. I don't even like thinking about it. Makes me queasy. Worse, it makes me think of the worst things that have ever happened to me. Like losing my Mom, or when I nearly OD'd, or the time I tried to end myself.

[PS] How do you think this song came out of an amplifier when it wasn't the song being played?

[JR] Beats me. I thought maybe it was picking up interference, like a signal from a local radio station or something. Didn't matter though. Kerry killed it, and then Erich nearly killed Kerry. I've seen him mad a hundred times, but nothing like the way he was that day. Even when Joss and me tried to break them up, Erich looked like all he wanted to do was end her. It all stopped when she broke his nose, because no matter how tough he always thought he was, Kerry was tougher. He kinda came back to himself after that, and we decided to leave him alone to think things over. That's when he disappeared. For about, I don't know a year or so. You know that part.

[PS] The label said he was in rehab.

[JR] Damage control. They had to say something. He wasn't in rehab. Nobody knew where he was, and the band was as good as dead after that. New album just released, and he decides to go AWOL? Yeah, nobody was happy. When they canceled the tour, sales started to flag, and the label had been heavily invested in the album. It was supposed to be their *Nevermind*, a real game-changer. But it was dead in the water. The death knell came when Joss started doing guest bass for other bands. That's never good, but he had to pay the bills, y'know? Kerry started drumming for The Pumps, and I'd never seen her happier, even though I know her heart was broken over Erich. They'd been talking marriage and shit and then he just vanishes? Even if he reappeared, it was over, man. Everything was.

[PS] And he did reappear.

[JR] Yeah. About two weeks ago. A Friday night. I was at home. He called. I was like "Dude! Where you been? Everyone's mad as hell at you." He ignored me. Said "Come to the house." I don't know where Kerry and Joss were at the time, but all of us were summoned to Erich's house on Galena Hill. He said he wanted to show us something exciting. Joss didn't show. Found out after he told Erich he was done and Erich could go fuck himself. Kerry's car was parked outside when I arrived, but she was already inside. As soon as I went into that house, I gagged. Place smelled like stale sweat and puke and shit and something else, like damp or mold. It was hard to breathe without feeling like you were pulling something toxic into your lungs, like that black shit miners get from being underground too long. I left the door open behind me just to let some air in, but it didn't seem to make much difference. It was like the fresh air didn't want to come in or couldn't.

[PS] There have been a lot of conflicting accounts about what was inside that house.

[JR] I've had time to think about that, and while I'm telling it straight, I think if ten people went into that house, they'd all have seen something different.

[PS] There's talk of psychotropic drugs and hallucinogens.

[JR] Could be, and sure as hell wouldn't have been the first time. All I know is what I saw, and what I saw made no sense at all. Like, really bizarre shit.

[PS] Can you describe it for me?

[JR] I can try, but you're the writer. I'm just a roadie. Never even finished high school.

[PS] Just tell me in your own words.

[JR] They were in the living room. Kerry and Erich. She was sitting on a milk crate, head down, a bottle of tequila in her hand. She was weaving, which told me she'd been hitting it kind of hard before she even got to the house. The coffee table was on its side, glass top shattered and scattered all over the rug, which had some kind of weird fungus thing growing underneath that had turned up the corner on one side. Everything Erich had once had on his walls: the framed photographs of him with all the bands they'd met and played with, those were all smashed on the floor. Same with the gold and platinum records. Just...everything in pieces. And while I can't be sure, I think he'd smeared shit all over the walls. There was this weird greenish fog hanging low over everything, like we were in a marsh, and not a ranch house on the outskirts of L.A.

[PS] And Erich?

[JR] Naked as the day he was born and so thin his ribs were pressing against his skin like coat hangers. His eyes...I don't know how to describe them. There, but gone, I guess. I've seen plenty of lunatics in my time. This business draws them. The loons and strung-out hangers-on. But this was something else. Eyes like black holes. He had his guitar in his hand, and there was some kind of green gunk all over it, moss and little mushrooms growing on the frets. All the strings were snapped and jangling around. He grinned when he saw me, and that's when I noticed half his teeth were missing. The few he still had were yellow and green. "Come in, Charlie," he said, and I had to look behind me to see who he was talking to, because I don't know anyone called Charlie. When I did, something behind me seemed to step into the wall, as if excusing itself from being seen. Freaked me the fuck out. "Come on now," Erich said. "Come listen." The amp was behind him, or at least some monstrous thing inspired by the old crooked amp we'd seen in rehearsal. This one was much, much bigger. Ten times the size at least. It took up one whole wall and appeared to have been built or forced into the stucco. Would have made a cool visual for an album cover, but I was terrified by it. That same ugly growth was all over it, like Erich had dragged it out of a swamp.

"You okay?" I asked, but I was looking at Kerry.

When she raised her head, I wished she hadn't. Her eyes, ears and nose were covered with crusted blood, and one of her pupils was bigger than the other. She grinned at me and her mouth made her face look small. "You should listen," she said. "We're going to bring the house down." She laughed then, and it was too high-pitched, too girly to come out of the tomboy I'd known my whole life.

"I've never been so inspired, so fucking creative," Erich yelled, his hair stuck to his skull with sweat or something else. "This is true art, man. You must hear it."

But I didn't want to. He strapped on the guitar with no strings and angled his hand as if to thrash a chord and I knew without knowing how, that he was going to be able to play it, that somehow the speaker was going to bellow out some hideous thing that would turn my brain to mush and drive me as mad as it had Kerry. And I couldn't do it. I turned to leave and the door was gone.

[PS] What do you mean?

[JR] I mean...gone. The hall, the door...they just weren't there anymore. It was just a wall, old and cracked and covered with more of that green mold, as if it had always been that way. When I turned back, Erich was looking at me with such lunatic hatred, it paralyzed me. Sure, we've had our issues. I even quit once when the cocaine started making a prick of him and he was impossible to be around, but I always came back because I loved him, loved them all. This was something new, and royally fucked up. He looked like he wanted to kill me, and that might not even be enough. So I just stood there because I didn't know what else to do, even though instinct told me to grab Kerry and find the nearest exit, one that hadn't magically disappeared.

[PS] Official word is he had a breakdown. Kerry too. That they'd been doing their weight in drugs that day.

[JR] Maybe, but *I* wasn't.

[PS] Kerry admitting herself to rehab afterward seems to support the story.

[JR] Kerry's not in rehab. She's in a mental institution.

[PS] Can I quote you on that? On the record?

[JR] Sure, I don't care. It'll come out sooner or later anyway.

[PS] Back to that night.

[JR] Yeah, it gets a bit hazy after that. Erich played some kind of song that wasn't a song at all. More like a bunch of mad people screaming in another room. Shook the fucking house. Thought it was gonna bring it down. And then Erich threw his head back, black eyes shut, legs set in a rocker pose, right leg out in front of him, bent at the knee, left leg bracing the floor behind him, dead straight. You know the one. And he raises his hand and I see what he's holding between the thumb and index finger of his playing hand. A tooth. One of his own, I guess, but he's using it as a pick on a guitar with no strings. And so he thrashes that power chord anyway and the floor rises like something under us is trying to come up through it. And then Erich's chest...Jesus Christ, man. I don't know if I can even talk about this.

[PS] Try.

[JR] Well, his fuckin' chest just opened like a shark's mouth, his broken ribs like teeth trying to gnash the strap off his guitar. I could see his insides, his heart and lungs, all of it black as night. My instinct was to help him, but what the fuck was I gonna do? It was like a grenade had gone off inside him, and anyway, he didn't look like he even needed help because he just kept playing, the ground kept shaking like a whale was about to...what do you call it when they jump out of the sea?

[PS] Breach?

[JR] Yeah, like that. I was scared, man, and Kerry kept laughing and giggling like it was some kind of prank. And then she looked at me with those weird eyes and her face looked ready to slide off her skull like a wet mask, and I screamed. I mean, I think I did. It was hard to tell because of all the screaming coming from everywhere else. And then I saw the amp. Looked like a great big dungeon door now, flexing and contracting in time with Erich's lungs, and I knew, in minutes, seconds, something was going to burst through it the same way something was going to come up through the floor, and when that happened, we, and probably the whole world, was gonna be royally fucked.

[PS] What did you do?

[JR] Only thing I could think of. I grabbed Kerry's bottle of tequila and threw it at the amp. Soaked that fucker. And it shuddered. *Shuddered*, like skin will when you douse it in ice water. Then I ran and the carpet tried to suck me down into the floor, turned to straight up glue. Even took one of my shoes. But I kept going. Took my lighter out of one pocket, my notebook of song lyrics out of the other, and lit it. Tossed my arm back to throw it, and Erich hit another chord. The amp bellowed like some deep-sea thing and suddenly I was a kid again with my stepfather doing things he shouldn't and my mother pretending he wasn't and I cried and felt my head crack and...is it okay to have a drink? What am I asking you for? It's my crib. Want one?

[PS] No thanks.

[JR] I saw every bad thing, so many bad things from my life, and some from Erich's and Kerry's too. Kerry never forgave herself for having a kid and giving it up for adoption when she was 17. Every day, she thought about that kid out there in the world and it made her want to die. The father was an abusive piece of shit who she left after he tried to strangle her. And Erich. Erich was a happy kid until his parents got killed in a car crash. It made him an introvert and the PTSD never left, because he was supposed to be on the trip with his parents but he didn't want to go, so, at age 14, he told them to go fuck themselves, and I guess they took his advice and fucked themselves right into the back of a semi. He got, as people would say, "weird" as if that's an insult anymore. He abandoned his faith, experimented with drugs, joined a band, and tried to kill himself more than once. Like me, Kerry and Erich were all kinds of fucked up. Tortured by the things they'd done or hadn't done. I suppose that's why we were drawn to one another, that feeling that something inside us was missing, something only other broken people could understand. We were tied together by the music, and now that had gone bad too. I saw it all, and it made my brain feel like Erich's black heart, like the door, flexing and contracting. I went blind and fell to my knees, but at some point, somehow, I touched the lighter to the amp. I know because I felt the heat. And I know because I heard it scream.

[PS] You must know how this all sounds.

[JR] Course I do. It's completely nuts. Like a bad acid trip. But it's what happened, or at least, what my brain is telling me happened, maybe to protect me, because if I'd really seen the truth, I'd have ripped my tongue out like Kerry did.

[PS] How did you manage to get out of there?

[JR] All I remember is feeling something like someone sticking a needle in both my ear drums and I went deaf. Then I passed out. When I woke up, I was lying on the grass outside with Kerry in my arms. She was unconscious too. And Joss was there, white as a ghost, bent over and vomiting into the dirt. He showed up after all. Just in time to save our asses. We piled into his car and got the hell out of there.

[PS] And Erich?

[JR] Dunno. House went up in smoke, so have to assume he did too.

[PS] But there was no body.

[JR] No. Some people are saying the heat was enough to vaporize him.

[PS] Is that what you think?

[JR] I don't know what happened to him. Nothing good, probably.

[PS] And what about some fans' claims that they've heard from him?

[JR] People still claim they see Elvis and Cobain, so I don't pay any attention to that. Idols are hard to let go. Some people never do.

[PS] Did you know Erich recorded a demo?

[JR] What are you talking about? When?

[PS] Hard to know for sure. Lot of speculation out there, but Steve Alwin, the producer, says he worked on it with Erich for a while until Alwin got an inner ear infection and had to bow out. From there, it's assumed Erich finished it himself the year he went missing.

[JR] I didn't know anything about that, but I'm glad we'll never get to hear it.

[PS] Why do you say that? Fans are clamoring for new tracks now that he's presumed dead.

[JR] Nobody should listen to that demo. Nobody will ever be the same again if they do. I'm glad it burned up.

[PS] It didn't though.

[JR] What?

[PS] Maybe the original did, but copies were received by what we must assume was every music magazine and radio station in the country at midnight last night.

[JR] That's not funny, man. Not at all.

[PS] I know it isn't. They'll play the whole thing in its entirely tonight as part of a nationwide tribute to Erich.

[JR] We have to stop it. We have to, do you understand?

[PS] Why would you want to do that?

[JR] Have you heard anything I've said? It'll kill everyone who hears it.

[PS] But I've heard it, and I'm still here.

[JR] You don't get it. You're not listening to me. That music is dangerous.

[PS] You don't celebrate the fact that Erich is going to accomplish what he set out to do?

[JR] And what was that?

[PS] Same thing every musician wants.

[JR] The fuck is wrong with your eyes, man?

[PS] He's going to bring the house down.

ABOUT THE AUTHOR

Hailed by Booklist as "one of the most clever and original talents in contemporary horror," Kealan Patrick Burke was born and raised in Ireland and emigrated to the United States a few weeks before 9/11. Since then, he has written five novels, among them the popular southern gothic slasher KIN, and over two hundred short stories and novellas, including BLANKY and THE HOUSE ON ABIGAIL LANE, both of which are currently in development for film and TV.

A five-time Bram Stoker Award-nominee, Burke won the award in 2005 for his coming-of-age novella THE TURTLE BOY, the first book in the acclaimed Timmy Quinn series.

As editor, he helmed the anthologies NIGHT VISIONS 12, TAVERNS OF THE DEAD, and QUIETLY NOW, a tribute anthology to one of Burke's influences, the late Charles L. Grant.

Most recently, he completed a new novel, MR. STITCH, a collection entitled GUESTS for Suntup Editions, and adapted SOUR CANDY for John Carpenter's NIGHT TERRORS series of graphic novels.

Kealan is represented by Merrilee Heifetz at Writers House and Kassie Evashevski at Anonymous Content.

He lives in Ohio with a Scooby Doo lookalike rescue named Red. Visit him on the web at www.kealanpatrickburke.com

Printed in Great Britain
by Amazon